Pen State
to
State Pen

Pen State
to
State Pen

CORNELL RICHARDS

Library of Congress Control Number:		2021916309
ISBN:	Hardcover	978-1-6641-8902-7
	Softcover	978-1-6641-8901-0
	eBook	978-1-6641-8900-3

Print information available on the last page.

Rev. date: 08/30/2021

To order additional copies of this book, contact:
Xlibris
844-714-8691
www.Xlibris.com
Orders@Xlibris.com
831565

CONTENTS

ACKNOWLEDGMENTS

I RIGHTFULLY ACKNOWLEDGE God first for breathing his breath in my lungs and providing me the opportunity to be consistent with my craft. I'm eternally grateful for the gifts that he has provided for me such as my parents Beverly and Altamonte Anderson. My little sister Trishawna Anderson, who will be the better version of myself in due time. World watch out for her! Much respect goes to Xlibris Publishing for giving not only myself but granting some brilliant, underappreciated writers a different route to get our stories heard. To Carl Anderson, great job on the cover. To Shanell Chann, thank you for helping to get this story in the hands of readers. To Janet Haywood, thank you for all of your contributions, Carmen London, Chevelle Howard, Jamahl Browne, Pam Finney, Damien, and Candice Jones, what a beautiful family. Ms. Janise, thank you for allowing me to be a part of your distribution of blessing the entire neighborhood with those beautiful flowers on Sundays. To Michelle Brooks, I truly appreciate your wisdom and guidance throughout this process. To Calvary Baptist Church. Pastor Garth Gittens, thank you for the tremendous blessings and for the powerful messages every Sunday. To Deacon Tauheed Adens, thank you for welcoming me into the church and for the great conversations and encouragement. To Theresa Brown, I'm super appreciative for all that you've done and for believing in me. To my writing partners, Marcelle Lofton, and James Robinson Jr., thank you for sticking with me. Our hard work will certainly pay off. To Dana Johnson and Stephanie Dunstan, thank you for the support. Mr. Kenny, Anthony, and Kenny. (My brothers for life). Mike, my barber, thanks for all the sharp haircuts. I certainly can't forget my brothers, Jamal McCants, Marland Doyle, James Paige, Keemo, and my entire Dewey Street Family. I hope all is well. Shonn Bunn, keep up the great work with producing those awesome beats. Alexandria Riley, and her children. Thank you for the support. Jasmine Rogers, thank you for your efforts. Twink, keep your head up. To everyone on 66th street, Sheed, Mr. Larry, Justin, Eric, Darnell, Amber, Alvin, Ms. Karen, Ms. Peggy, Sahmeer, Poo, Mar, Ant and Chris. Sorry if I missed anyone. To all of the staff members at Volunteers of America in California on Broadway Place, Mr. Rich, Steve, Ms. Nunah, Ms. Frances, Damario, Jamiesha, The cook Mr. Anthony, Mr. Alex, Mr. Sherman, thanks for all the second plates of food. I remember that. To the guys that helped me out during my first and final state prison sentence. Tyson, Eric, Fred, Hoover, Tone, Mr. Maresca, and Mr. Schimdt. Hope all is well on your end.

CHAPTER 1

The Party's Over

I RECALL BEING a complete nuisance in the first grade by throwing crayons at my teacher Ms. Jones because she kept me in from recess. Overall, my teachers from John Barry Elementary School taught me some tremendous lessons but my angles were a bit off when using Ms. Jones's head for target practice. But after the crayons would hit the chalkboard, I would quickly hide my hand and snicker as Ms. Jones surveyed the class, attempting to catch the perpetrator. I had trouble reading and lashed out whenever the lenient, older, fat, white woman in room 104 corrected me, causing the other children to laugh. It was a beautiful, sunny day when she boastfully made the announcement in front of the class. "Cornell, you'll be staying in with me to work on your reading." But sitting by the window, watching the other children play was the most treacherous reprimand for any child. After struggling enormously on my own with pronouncing a few minor words, I quickly began to plot my most inevitable revenge. Ms. Jones often used thumbtacks when placing the other student's work on the wall to display their achievements, which fueled me even more to accomplish the reprisal. I knew that she wouldn't instantly return after taking the children to the schoolyard and more than likely she would seek refuge in the teacher's lounge, smoking cigarettes. That was just enough time for me to run over to her desk, steal a thumbtack and place it on her chair. The plan was splendid because she spent so much time in the lounge, that she completely forgot about tutoring me. She finally returned along with the rest of the class and continued with our studies. When the children were seated, she loudly apologized to me for losing track of time. "Cornell, I'm so sorry honey, we'll have to do it again tomorrow." I gave no reply, but was filled with excitement and patiently waited for her to be inflicted with the same pain she imposed, for denying me the anxious delight. She paced around giving instructions then mentioned, "My feet are killing me," which prepared me for her agonizing outburst that surely frightened the class but was certainly to my amusement after she pulled out her chair and unknowingly sat on the thumbtack. "OOUUCH."

Restraining my laughter was impossible and was a dead giveaway that I was the culprit. She quickly wobbled over to me while rubbing her buttocks as the other children snickered. She began to scold me while pointing her finger in my face. "Cornell Richards, you are absolutely terrible; I can't deal with you." I was completely unfazed as she then dragged me out of the classroom by my left ear. "Let's go, you little Nigger." She then bit her bottom lip, indicating regret for her poor choice of words. I knew exactly where she was taking me. It wasn't to Principal Shorter's office, who was an African American female, easily manipulated pushover, who thought I was so cute and would have given me a popsicle. Ms. Jones took me to room 102. The authoritarian, no-nonsense Ms. Dalton was a much older, black woman, who looked straight out of the '70s with her long dresses decorated with flowers. Her shoulders were often covered with a sweater, and she sported thick black reading glasses with the chain hanging on the side. Ms. Dalton was every child's nightmare and maintained a dominating presence. Right after she answered the door, Ms. Jones immediately confessed, "Take him, I'm about to lose my religion and my job." "What did he do this time?" Ms. Dalton asked. With her face bloodshot red, Ms. Jones unhanded me then replied, "Let him tell you what he did." Ms. Dalton stared me down, providing me with the opportunity to speak. I instantly admitted, "I put a thumbtack on her chair," then I burst out laughing. Ms. Dalton just shook her head then relieved Ms. Jones of her duties. "Ok, I got him." Elementary School was some time ago, but I remember precisely the feeling when walking into the room, packed with other focused and well-behaved first graders. There was little lighting in the room as Ms. Dalton sat me at a desk in the corner and said, "Little boy, you're either going to end up at Pen State or the State Pen." It turned out that I ended up going to both. Due to the incalculable amount of prayers and support from both of my parents Mr. and Mrs. Anderson that I managed to elude any serious trouble with the law. Their efforts were complemented with the assistants of my grandparents, Mr. and Mrs. Gray, and of course I'll pat myself on the back for capitalizing after having such a tremendous support system. So years later, on a warm spring evening, we all stayed home to have a family dinner celebrating my college graduation. My mom was thrilled and continued to ramble as we ate. "Look at you, look at you, I'm so proud of my baby. Here, have some more corn." "Thanks, mom," I glady replied. My little sister Trish felt the need to remind me of a childhood torture. "Is it true that the kids used to call you Corny Cornell because you ate so much corn?" "Mom, tell her to leave me alone or no Wi-Fi for three months." "Trish, don't tease your brother, as a matter of fact, here's some more vegetables." Pops was a bit quiet but always showed concern. "So, you have that big job interview on Monday morning at the Probation Office, right?" "Yup," "Great job son. Wow, you accomplished the American dream, a great job offer straight out of college." "Thanks pop, yeah so, I'll just chill out for the weekend and get ready for the interview on Monday." "Ok, sounds like a plan," he replied. That was actually my intention but I figured, hey, I just spent the last four years trying to achieve the biggest accomplishment in my life and a little celebration wouldn't hurt. I called up my white college friend Lloyd, who I met during freshman year, and my neighborhood knuckled head friend Kenny, who was black and I always tried to keep him under my wing. He would often get into all types of crap, from petty theft, drugs, and he even stole a few of the neighbor's cars in our Overbrook neighborhood.

When I called to tell him about the party he was thrilled. "Hey Ken, you missed my graduation ceremony, but there's a party tonight at the school. Let's go." "My fault Nell, I totally forgot man, but yeah I was bored to death, is it going to be some white girls there?" "Ha-ha, I believe so" "Hell yeah, let's go." I then contacted Lloyd to confirm he'd be at the party. "Hey Lloyd, dumb question but are you going to the graduation party tonight?" He arrogantly replied, "Am I going? Bro, I'm already here, there are drinks and naked ass everywhere. Chicks are getting lit." Lloyd wasn't too fond of Kenny for obvious reasons and I knew he would object. "Ok cool, hey, I'm going to bring Kenny, he doesn't have much to do." "Oh no man, not that guy, I'm pretty sure he'll find some drama to get into." "But if he's with us, that won't be the case." "I guess, ok see you guys when you get here." My folks were asleep when I was heading out, and I didn't want to wake them. It was eighty degrees but Kenny was wearing a black hoodie when we met each other at the bus stop. "Bro, you're not going to need that hoodie; it's going to be pretty hot in there." "I'm going to be freezing, sitting on the bus for this long ass ride." The bus finally arrived and we got to the party an hour later. We entered the dorm with the sounds of Drake blasting, "I'm on One." Lloyd was happy to see me as we greeted each other with a series of handshakes that certainly made Kenny feel left out. As usual, Lloyd was thrilled to see me, "About time bro, you made it." Lloyd then yelled at Kenny, "Hey you, stay out of trouble." Kenny ignored him then quickly vanished into a dark, smokey room, filled with intoxicated girls. As I poured some fruit punch that was spiked with only God knows what, I felt someone pat me on my ass. It was Vanessa, "Hey there handsome, is this for me?" She then snatched the drink out of my hand. We had dated off and on over the years. Vanessa was gorgeous. She was Jamaican with Indian hair and had a peanut butter complexion. We danced for a bit, then Lloyd jumped in the middle of us and began taking pictures and screaming "Congratulations to us, Woooo." After a few more drinks, Vanessa was dragging me back to her dorm. I saw Lloyd in his room getting oral sex and smiling from ear to ear. Minutes later, I began smiling as well when Vanessa removed her t-shirt and ripped jeans. I quickly snatched off her panties and plunged into her. I was so confused; I couldn't make up my mind whether I wanted to continue thrusting or tasting her, as she moaned intensely whenever I did both. She then reminded me that she would be leaving for London to study abroad for her Master's Degree. "Don't go falling in love with me, pretty boy, maybe I'll get lucky enough and meet one of those dashing Englishmen." "Yeah, to show them how insane you really are hahaha." Suddenly, our kissing and laughter were frighteningly interrupted when several shots rang out. "POW POW POW POW POW!! We could hear people screaming and trampling over each other trying to escape the horror. Vanessa and I rolled off the bed and I covered her until the coast seemed to be clear. The shots came from Lloyd's room, so I quickly ran over to check on him. When approaching the door, I saw his quivering body riddled with bullets as he held on for dear life. The girl he was with just kept screaming instead of calling the paramedics, which she eventually did as I tried CPR. The medics finally arrived and pushed me out of the way and I bumped into Kenny. He seemed a bit petrified but I thought he was just shaken up because of the incident. He asked, "Nell, are you ok?" "Yeah, I'm good, Lloyd just got shot but I don't know what happened. I'm going to find out which hospital they're taking him to." He stated the obvious then strangely asked, "Hey, it's hot in here, isn't your locker nearby?" "I told you that you wouldn't need to bring that thing anyway, give it to me and wait here. I'll just hurry up and throw it in my locker and we can get it on the way back." "Ok cool." On the way to my locker, I looked in Vanessa's room and wasn't surprised to see that she had taken off. I threw Kenny's hoodie in my locker then ran back to catch up with him but he was gone. I thought maybe he'd gotten lost, so I texted and called him but there was no answer. I didn't want to leave him stranded but I was more concerned about Lloyd. Luckily, he was transported to a nearby hospital not too far from the school, so whenever I got in contact with Kenny, I would tell him to just meet me there. I sat in the waiting area all night with Lloyd's parents Mr. and Mrs. Perkins until a mid-age, balding, doctor wearing glasses came out and gave us the news that

Lloyd had died from multiple gunshot wounds. "I'm sorry, we tried the best we could but his injuries were just too severe. I'm really sorry." Mrs. Perkins immediately began to cry as her husband consoled her. The police arrived and addressed Lloyd's parents. Detective Grant was a taller, dark hair, white male, that favored Judge Alex. His partner, Detective Simmons was short and white and whose breath smelled like garbage.

Detective Grant offered his condolences to the family. "Mr. and Mrs. Perkins I'm terribly sorry about what happened to your son, and I promise we'll do everything we can to get justice." Mrs. Perkins couldn't even respond; she just broke down as Mr. Perkins said "Thank you," while also sobbing. I then introduced myself to the Detectives. "I'm Cornell. I'm a friend of Lloyd's. We were celebrating tonight." Simmons then asked to speak with me. I didn't have anything to hide, and hell yeah, I wanted them to catch the killer. Before speaking with them, I texted my mom, letting her know that I was cool but waited until I got home to tell her what happened. Both detectives walked me outside and Simmons asked, "So where were you at the time of the shooting?" "I was with a friend in her room, hanging out for a bit. But she left for London but you can check the cameras, her name is Vanessa." "Ok," Grant said. Simmons added, "We're sorry about your friend but we might need you to help us." I confidently replied, "Sure whatever you guys need." When they left, I called Kenny again and he finally answered. "Hey Nell, I had to get out of there, it was too much going on." "Yeah, I understand. Are you home?" I asked, "Yeah, I just got here," "Ok the bus should be here pretty soon," "Ok bro be safe." When the bus finally arrived, the driver gave me a crazy look, as I was covered in blood. I walked past a few passengers that oddly gazed at me and I just sat in the back, completely horrified about what happened to my friend. I got home around 3 am and immediately changed clothes and took a shower. Still, in disbelief, I managed to fall asleep but was awoken a few hours later with a knock at the door by my mother. "Cornell, what the hell is going on? I saw on the news that there was a shooting at the school. Are you ok?" "Yeah mom, but my friend Lloyd was killed, I managed to make it out. I got in pretty late last night and didn't want to wake you and Pops." "Oh son, I'm sorry to hear that. Thank God, you made it out safely. I can't imagine what that boy's poor mother must be going through." Pops then entered my room. "Are you ok son?" "Yeah, I'm ok." "Well come on downstairs and get something to eat."

Although I was grieving, I could tell that Pops still wanted me to watch the basketball highlights on ESPN with him. Watching the highlights with Pops did in fact help until the unexpected happened. There was a hard knock on the door and we knew that it wasn't a family member. Whoever it was they meant business. When I opened the door with Pops breathing on the back of my neck, Detective Grant and Detective Simmons were standing on my porch. Grant didn't hesitate, "Mr. Richards you're under arrest." I shockingly replied, "Under arrest for what?" He answered, "We'll read you your rights and charges at the police station." My mom ran out on the porch and my family just helplessly watched along with the nosey neighbors, as I was hauled off to the local precinct. They sat me in a room by myself, handcuffed to the chair then Simmons told me to sit tight. Minutes later, they both returned with Grant reading me my rights and charges. "Cornell Richards, you're being charged with possession of an illegal firearm, and concealing a deadly weapon that committed a homicide, which is a second-degree felony." I exploded. "What the hell are you talking about?" "What deadly weapon? And I didn't hide anything from you. I told your stupid ass that I was with a friend of mine in her room at the time of the shooting." Simmons answered, "We understand that college boy, that's why you're not being charged with murder. We checked the cameras like you insisted and got a search warrant for everyone's locker. Everyone was clean except for yours.

The bullets that were found inside Lloyd's body belonged to the gun that was found inside your locker wrapped in a black hoodie. We have you on camera stashing it inside your locker, then quickly fleeing the scene and jumping on the bus after you briefly spoke with us, trying to make yourself look like a concerned, grieving friend.

You're a little piece of shit, I should crack your damn skull for trying to play us." I boldly replied, "Do it, do it, you stinking ass cracker. I didn't do anything." Simmons grabbed me by the collar and roughed me up but he was quickly restrained by his partner. "It's ok," Grant said, "We'll get our day in court." They booked me, then tossed me two cheese sandwiches which I immediately inhaled because I was starving. Stale bread and cheese never tasted so good along with a baby box of orange juice. As I sat on the ground in the pissy cell, my mind ran rapidly with questions and confusion. Like, why the hell would Kenny shoot Lloyd but more importantly, Simmons came back to tease me. "Hey college boy, that chick you said you were with; the hallway was too dark, so we couldn't see you going into the room and the person is unrecognizable on the camera. Furthermore, you said she already left for London and she can't be expedited back here because she's not a suspect, so there goes your alibi dickhead. Get comfortable Richards, you're going to be here for a while." I just knew that once Kenny heard what happened to me, he would confess that I had no knowledge of the gun being inside the hoodie and I would be freed. What a start! My friend had just lost his life after graduating college and I missed out on a great job opportunity. It got better, I was denied bail because the prosecutor mentioned that I had a friend in London and that I could be a flight risk. My parents once again sat miserably helpless in the courtroom as the D.A prepared to melt everything that I've worked incredibly hard to achieve. After waiting two weeks for Kenny to turn himself in, I finally realized that was wishful thinking, so I took action and requested to speak with the idiot detectives. They came to see me about a week later and I told them that the hoodie belonged to Kenny. Grant replied, "We found out what happened at the party. Kenny tried to hit on the same girl that Lloyd was with, in the room. Witnesses say that Lloyd humiliated Kenny by calling him a loser in front of everyone and said that he didn't belong there." That's when Lloyd took the girl in the room and Kenny retaliated by simply shooting him several times."

Simmons added, "Such nice friends, you've got there, Richards." I sat there shocked and speechless. Simmons continued, "Kenny is

8

on the run for murder but we still got you on the hook for hiding the gun in the locker. So, that will give the family some sort of closure and expose you as an accomplice with their son's murder." I honestly replied, "But I'm telling you the truth, I didn't know that a gun was in his hoodie." They looked at each other, then Grant replied "That's for your lawyer to prove. Take care kid." During the trial, all parties were in attendance. My family sat on one side of the courtroom and Lloyds family sat on the other. I was able to get a mediocre attorney, who just mentioned the basics that Lloyd and I were good friends and I couldn't have any knowledge of a gun being inside the hoodie. The vicious prosecutor easily sacked our minimal defense by showing the video of Kenny and me talking in the hallway after the smoke cleared and him giving me the hoodie. Truthfully, the video looked pretty convincing, and if I was a juror, I wouldn't believe a word that came from my attorney's mouth. The jurors came back with a verdict in two hours. The Judge asked them to read it, and I was found guilty in the second degree for illegal gun possession and concealing a deadly weapon that committed a homicide. About a month later at the sentencing, my attorney said that because I had no prior criminal record, the D.A would still recommend four years in a state penitentiary, which was their original plea offer. I recall my mother fainting and Lloyd's mother screaming out, "Four years? That's all that black bastard gets for helping to kill my son?"

I remained at the county jail, specifically in a unit for inmates awaiting transportation to the state penitentiary. I briefly had a cell to myself which looked like an efficiency apartment. During that time, I heard all of the jail stories from other inmates about prison riots and the most infamous question upon arrival, "Where would you like your body to be sent in case you were to be killed?" That certainly didn't sit too well with me. But I knew much better than to believe everything I heard in prison. I didn't even believe everything that I heard on the street. My conscience told me that I would not have a rough ride during this prison sentence. I was a victim of circumstance but clearly, this would be a very interesting experience and maybe some sort of lesson to be learned. The possibilities of me meeting some really great people were high. A few hours later I heard my door buzz and I jumped off the bed. A slender white guy by the name of Mike entered my room. His company arrived right on time as I began to feel a little lonely. He had just pleaded guilty to a burglary charge and was also awaiting transportation. More importantly, Mike was cool and seemed to be very knowledgeable about the type of prison where I would be doing my sentence. "Cornell, don't worry, you're going to be fine. You're going to one of those college campus jails." Confused, I asked, "What do you mean, college campus jails?" He confidently answered, "This is your first time and you have no prior record, the jail you'll be going to is a recently built facility, it will look like a college campus. The food is delicious, they give you nice clean clothes, big fluffy pillows so you can be really comfortable and keep coming back." We both laughed. But he admitted, "Now me on the other hand, I'm a repeat violent offender. I'm going to one of those older, castle-like jails where the C.O (Correctional Officer) stands in a tower with a shotgun, and crazy barb-wires everywhere, typical maximum security." I tried to doubt him. "Not necessarily," He smirked then replied, "Nell, I broke into a woman's house looking for jewels. She saw me, she looked me right in the eye then called me Mikey-O." I couldn't help but laugh as he continued, "So when the D.A offered me a plea deal of only 18 months, I quickly signed the paper in ten different places, giving up all my rights before they changed their minds because, with my criminal history, I surely deserve at least 10-12 years." With that statement, I was convinced that Mike knew his stuff but it was still up in the air where I would be transferred. With this type of criminal justice system, maybe our destinations would be the complete opposite of what Mike predicted?

CHAPTER 2

State of Mind

IT WAS LATE August when our door buzzed in the afternoon. Mike and I awoke from our naps and were summoned by the unit counselor, a mid-age heavyset black guy by the name of Mr. Pierce. We momentarily stood in the hallway, until our names were called and Mike went in first. He quickly returned with his face red and tears gushing. I assumed reality had made its mark about his destination but it was another issue. Mike was summoned to the counselor's office because his mother had died. I didn't know what to do as he stood in the hallway cursing loudly, of course out of anger but Mike mentioned that he wanted to kill himself, so two correctional officers restrained him and escorted him to the suicide unit. I never saw Mike again. When I walked into the office, there was a brief pause from Mr. Pierce which scared me half to death because I thought he was going to tell me that my mother had also died. Trust and believe, I would have turned that entire facility upside down and restraining the correctional officers. Pierce just needed to catch his breath before stating, "Sorry about that Mr. Richards, these things are never easy, telling someone that their loved one has passed away but as you expected, you'll be transferred to a state penitentiary tomorrow." I'm from West Philadelphia, so I'm naturally tough. But honestly, I was a tad bit scared due to fear of the unknown. Mr. Pierce then asked, "Are you alright?" I nervously answered, "Yeah, I'm cool." He then informed me, "So, you're allowed to make a phone call right now, I'm assuming it's going to be to mother?" I declined the opportunity to make the call. I was doing well by staying cool, calm, and collected and didn't want to break down, and getting emotional over the phone while speaking to my mother. Especially not in front of Mr. Pierce's beautiful brunette assistant. Pierce then instructed, "Ok Mr. Richards, just return back to your cell and pack all of your necessary paperwork, and good luck."

I closed his office door then took a deep breath just to mentally prepare myself for the next stage of the journey. It was around 5 am in the morning when two correctional officers escorted me and about twenty other inmates to a huge garage. A Lieutenant, wearing a white shirt, was a white, mid-age guy with salt and pepper hair and spoke forcefully when giving instructions. "Ok gentleman, rise and shine, take your head out of your ass, and listen up. I'm going to be calling your first and last name along with two initials afterward. Those initials are marked on the brown bags on the table. Inside the bags is your breakfast. The initials stand for the state prison you'll be transported to. So simply grab the bag with the correct initials after I call your name. Of course, a few people messed up, as one guy asked. "Does it really matter which bag we grab we're still going to jail?" Another guy felt the need to answer him. "Yeah, you idiot, it does, maybe some of us have a different type of breakfast prepared in the bag. We can tell that you surely didn't use your head when committing your crime." The other guy replied, "Well that makes two of us because we have the same letters on our bags." We all laughed. As the other gentleman sat there with a stupid look on his face. My name was called next followed by the letters CT. I then asked a white guy sitting next to me, "What the hell does CT stand for?" "I'm not sure, but it may be really far away." We all then boarded an old school bus that was painted dark gray and covered with a grill on both sides of the widows. While riding through areas that I never knew existed with both ankles and wrist shackled, I admired the small towns of Central Pennsylvania. The secluded well-kept landscaping was certainly to my liking. I then began to get upset about my four-year sentence, until I overheard two inmates behind me mention, "Man, they gave me 10-20," "Yeah, they gave me 20-40." A much older black guy, who sat in front of me looked as if he was old enough to be my grandfather had stated, "This is my second 30-year sentence." I grimaced. Hearing their misery immediately made me feel better because compared to them, I was basically already home, relaxing with my feet up. The driver seemed to be in a rush to get us to the prison but I got a glimpse of the nice, big houses. I wasn't expecting to have any visitors but the location was quite a distance. It took us just under several hours to reach our destination in a place called Coal Township.

Mike was absolutely correct. The place resembled a college campus, minus the barbed wire for obvious reasons. When we stepped off the bus two older, white C. O's began to unlock our shackles with one demanding, "Ok gentlemen, let's get you all some fresh gear." They both escorted all twenty of us to the inventory room. Another C.O demanded, "Next, go into that room and remove all of your clothes. I want to see dick and balls, and spread your cheeks." It was the most degrading experience in my life but a necessary process the C. O's had to conduct when checking for contraband. However, one inmate decided to express his frustration and said to the C.O, "You're just a little too enthused, this must be your favorite part of the day," After a little murmuring from the others, the C.O replied, "Well clearly, you're just as excited that's why you keep coming back here, now hurry up and get dressed, your new girlfriend will be waiting for you to braid his hair." I just shook my head and took a deep breath. I was then given three burgundy red uniforms along with a coat, and a skull hat with gloves as the winter was quickly approaching. One of the officers then called out our new ID names which were numbers and housing units. "LA5843, C building." That was my new name. Wow, I couldn't believe it. I went from being a promising, young professional, fresh out of college, to just another number being called. After looking at the others, who stood behind me, it resembled cattle being lined up for slaughter. I was then instructed by one of the officers, "Richards, walk straight up the path. That's where your unit will be." "Ok, thanks." While walking by myself, I immediately thought about running away. The fences weren't that high but I would have a little trouble with the barb-wires, never mind the possible wildlife that I was unequipped to handle. Of course, the stupid attempt would only add to my sentence, so that notion quickly passed. I saw how the correctional officers, for the most part, spoke to the inmates cordially and vice versa. I saw the inmates doing a great job with planting flowers along the walkway and how the inmates were keeping the facility clean. I saw inmates studying in classrooms. There were inmates exercising in both indoor and outdoor areas of the gym, and playing basketball as if they were trying to earn a spot in the NBA Draft. When approaching my housing unit, I opened the double doors and saw a two-level dorm-style setup, and a total of one-hundred inmates either sitting around watching television, playing cards, or reading the newspaper. It was basically a daycare center for adult males. As I stood at the main desk, using my peripheral vision, I saw a few inmates standing across and staring at me. Suddenly, there was a loud scream, "OOOCHH." Two African American inmates suddenly began stabbing and punching another black inmate as he struggled to defend himself. Several officers then ran over and restrained and escorted all parties out of the building. One officer yelled, "Over a damn bag of chips?" A heavy-set white, C.O then introduced himself to me. "I'm Officer Benson, you're upstairs in cell 214, Richards." "Ok thank you," I replied. My cellmate Stanley was a tall mid-age black guy with a disfigured nose and had salt and pepper hair. It was later that night after our showers that Stanley informed me that he was from Southwest Philadelphia. He graduated from Temple University, with a degree in Business Management. He then admitted, "Yeah man, I caught my girl cheating, so I beat that ass, I tried to kill that chick. They hit me with aggravated assault. Luckily this was my first major case, so they gave me only 4 years." Wow I thought, I wasn't surprised to hear that he trashed his girl, I was more fascinated that it was our first time in jail after we both earned college degrees. I then chuckled to myself, sparking his curiosity, "What are you laughing at?" I instantly replied, "Have you ever seen a white man go to court with a black lawyer?" After pondering, seconds later he burst out laughing, then answered, "I don't even recall seeing that in the movies, that's how you know the racial tension is still high within the court system." Later that night I began to wonder how many other people didn't start coming to jail until after graduating college? I then said to Stanley, "Well at least folks can still get their college degrees while they're here. He replied, "Nope they stopped that program a long time ago my young friend." "What do you mean? When I first got here, I saw those inmates studying." He corrected me with a smile "They were studying for their G.E.D. Good Enough Diploma. Hahaha." He continued, "In the early '90s a Sheriff assembled a town hall meeting, protesting that society is spending millions sending their kids to college but the government is giving the degrees away for free to criminals. There may be some programs that allow you to get college credits but for the most part, the system is geared towards the G.E.D program." The two worlds of the oppressed vs the affluent were extremely similar and I was willing to absorb all the jewels from my mishaps because clearly, God meant good from the evil that had fallen upon me. If my memory serves me correctly? It took exactly one week after arriving at Coal Township for me to decide to write this compelling tale and to create a catchy title. I basically wanted to expose how college life was very similar to jail life and which individuals had better opportunities after spending four years in both establishments.

We can begin with my arrival at college when I first met Lloyd. I was unpacking my clothes and straightening my side of the room when I saw him outside of our door, flirting with a long hair beauty and inviting several others to a painting party for all the freshman dorms. He was slightly arrogant, good-looking with dirty blond hair, he was simply the white version of myself. He introduced himself after getting a few phone numbers. "Hey, you must be my new roommate, I'm Lloyd," "Yeah, I'm Cornell, nice to meet you." He then suggested, "Hey, let's flip a quarter to see who gets which side of the room. When the quarter landed on heads, I was relieved because

I favored the right side of the room. He then informed me that "Nell, I'm having a painting party this Saturday, could use some touching up in here," as he looked around at the walls. I hated dorm-style living, I hated sharing space, not to mention a ninety-square-foot box with two beds. Similar to prison where there are two beds in a small room but with a metal toilet, that lacked privacy. That weekend Lloyd's party was a huge success but was a clear indication that he was more of a party animal and would not be a good fit for me. I later moved out and got my own apartment. I got a job through the work-study program, working in the library, checking student ID's and stacking away returned books. It was only supposed to be twenty hours a week but my supervisor Ms. Carol, a nice-looking mid-age, Jamaican woman, admitted, "You know it's actually less expensive to have you working than to hire a security guard, so if you want the extra shifts there yours. For your Behavior Health curriculum, you just have to maintain a C average." I was grateful. "Ok sure will. Thank you. Ms. Carol." So, I used my 10.50 hr., income to pay the rent for my studio apartment that was right off-campus. I was very fortunate and a lot more comfortable. The studio was only six hundred dollars a month with all utilities included. After being at Coal Township for only a couple of months, I was offered an opportunity to move into a dorm room that housed ten other inmates. A few of the guys were not getting along and knew that I was a quiet guy that stayed mostly to myself. I quickly declined. If I didn't tolerate one roommate in college, I surely wasn't going to abide having ten in prison and dealing with all that snoring and multiple personalities. Occupying my time was essential, so applying for the work program and getting a job in the kitchen was the best option. The kitchen job paid twelve cents an hour." It wasn't about the money because my parents always sent me money. But I wanted to make a difference and execute my nature of genuinely helping others. So, I forfeited my twelve-cent salary and applied for the volunteer program, tutoring the inmates for their G.E.D. I just needed to have my official college transcripts mailed to the facility. My mother was so proud. "Oh, absolutely son, I'm so proud of you that you're so concerned with others regardless of your circumstance. We're praying for you Cornell, mommy loves you." The transcripts arrived a week later and the position was mine. Ms. Foley, a short, older, white woman was the Lead Instructor and reminded me of my first-grade teacher Ms. Jones. Ms. Foley was glad to have me and was impressed that I had earned my degree when greeting me in the study room. "Nice to meet you Cornell, thank you for applying, it gets pretty hectic in here, so every little bit helps." I thought she was exaggerating but when the clock struck 9 am, the door swung open with about thirty hungry minds waiting to soak up all the knowledge. I briefly introduced myself, "Good morning everyone "I'm Cornell Richards and I'll be the new tutor, so I'm here to help, just simply ask." I helped a few students with English then had a moment of reflection about the vast number of college students in society that have the opportunity to study higher learning and were dropping out left and right.

During my lunch breaks, I started doing research on the percentage of inmates that obtained a college degree before getting arrested. It was sad but honestly, I felt a little special after seeing the article in a magazine that mentioned, "Not more than 5% or 6%." Along with my prison sentence, I also had mandatory programs levied by the judge during my sentencing. By the outer appearance of the white mid-age judge, he obviously had a drinking problem and was probably under the influence when sentencing me. I briefly entertained the thought of writing him a letter to ask, did he mean to say four months, instead of four years? But I feared he would reply with, in fact, I meant 14 years. With his rough voice and sagging facial features, he ordered me to take a Violence Prevention course and a Victim Awareness course. They were group sessions that were facilitated by a pretty blunt instructor named Mr. Phelps. "Look, I know that half of you guys are in here for a bunch of garbage anyway. You guys are supposed to be home, relaxing with a cold brew, with your girl, or with your guy. I guess that's the new thing now, I went to a basketball game the other night, while I was checking for the score, some gay faggots were checking for some guy's ass." If Phelps had made those comments on a college campus, he would have been terminated

17

without pay. Belligerent comments and discriminating against others for their sexual preference were prohibited in college but a bit casual in the prison classroom. But I had a few idiot professors in college. One in particular, who felt the need to issue a thirty-page assignment the first week of class and provide two weeks to have it completed. Serves me right for not utilizing my resources. Ratethisprofessor.com could have saved me the W grade (Withdrawal) on my transcript.

As it relates to dropping a course, I committed a pretty serious error in prison. It had been weeks since I had a haircut and maybe weeks until it was time for our housing unit to sign up for the barbershop. Prison, or no prison, I had an image to maintain. I had previously observed some of the other inmates cracking a razor then placing the blade in a fine-tooth comb then gently cutting their own hair. It looked pretty easy, so I gave it a try as Stanley laid on the bottom bunk, reading a magazine. It actually worked, nothing fancy, just a light trim. I finished just in time for dinner and simply placed the razor and blade on our desk table. Unknowingly, while at dinner the correctional officers did a routine, room check. I wasn't hiding anything because the blade was openly left on the table. But Officer Benson, with his beer belly, and who played by the book with specific inmates, wrote me up for altering the razor. He placed a pink slip under my door, once I returned from dinner. This was bad. I've seen Benson let other inmates slide on more serious issues and I had a few choice words for him once the doors opened and it was rec time. "Benson, what the hell is your problem? Why did you write me up for that stupid razor?" "Because you broke it. Maybe you were preparing to stab someone." "Benson, did I tell you that someone was bothering me?" "No, you didn't, but you've also been here long enough to know the rules kid. You're not allowed to alter the razor." I was furious and continued, "Benson, this could affect me at my parole hearing when it's decision time for me to go home. You could have easily given me the benefit of the doubt, and just threw it in the trash along with yourself." He shot me a look like he wanted to take my head off but he replied. "Well, it's out of my hands now, I already turned in my copy of the write-up, so you'll have a hearing with the housing coordinator. She'll decide what to do."

I was rightfully worried but Stanley said, "Yeah, you'll probably get cell restriction," "Cell Restriction, what's that?" "That means no activities like gym, or outside the yard. Oh, and that means you can't go to the classes while you're on cell restriction. If you miss a certain number of days, Phelps could drop you from the courses and you'll have to wait for months to get back in just to start all over again." I was pissed. I had about three months completed. Stanley advised me, "Don't worry, simply write Phelps a note letting him know what happened. He knows that some of the officers can be dickheads." I saw the housing coordinator a few days later. A mid-age white woman with long brown hair, wearing glasses. I didn't even catch her name. I just quickly admitted to wanting to cut my hair and she gave me a thirty-day cell restriction. God was good, the very next day after waking up from my nap, the C.O that was working slipped a response letter from Phelps under my door that read, "I'll leave the light on for you." I really appreciated Stanley's advice. But that wasn't the case in college, I was dropped five times for poor academic scholarship. In my freshman year, Lloyd and I partied like rock stars. He was doing coke with a red-light room full of girls and I smoked weed like a chimney with a few med students. That's how I met Vanessa. She first liked this corky white kid but he was too geeky. The other black guys were loud and obnoxious, so I simply stood alone in a corner sipping my beer, watching them make a fool of themselves. She asked me for a light. We drank, we smoked, we went back to her dorm and we broke her headboards. While laying in bed, she confirmed, "Quiet guys make the best lovers. But that dork was a little too quiet for me." "Well in his defense you are intimidating. He's probably not used to talking to girls like you." "Why because I'm black? Oh my gosh, I sound like a black guy." We both just laughed. Coincidentally, her aunt Ms. Carol was my supervisor in the library, so although I wasn't taking classes, I was still working and attending all the parties with Lloyd.

One night after spending the day cleaning my apartment, I looked at my failing grades and had a deep moment of reflection. Due to Hall of Fame Quarterback John Elway's countless number of last-minute heroics of come from behind wins, Super Bowl appearances, and victories, I'm convinced that he's certainly one of the greatest Quarterbacks of all time. But from watching the Mile-High Champion, I confused last-minute heroics with intentional procrastination. Elway didn't purposely wait until the fourth quarter to begin playing the game, it was mainly due to his opponent's failure to capitalize on opportunities to put the game away, and his constant refusal to quit along with inspiring his teammates with remarkable play. I failed to comprehend the fact that procrastination was hindering my attempts of being a successful college student. I often waited until the last minute to register for classes, or missed the deadline and had to wait for a student to drop out of a class due to lack of payment. All of which would be to my benefit towards pulling off a last-minute heroic.

CHAPTER 3

Cornell's University

COLLEGE WAS A tremendous journey. It's primarily a place for people to explore and to find out who they are and what's their purpose in life. I knew going in that I wanted to help others make better choices, so I studied Behavior Health/ Human Services. But to my surprise, some people on campus had no clue what they wanted to do. It was quite baffling. One naïve, white guy said to me while standing in line as we waited to register for classes, "I didn't even declare a major yet, but I'm just going to sign up for a bunch of classes. I gave him a blank stare then replied, "So you're about to waste a lot of money taking classes you possibly don't need then when you eventually do declare a major and you graduate, you'll complain about the enormous amount of debt that you now owe, ok nice." He replied, "Wow, I never thought of it that way." "Yeah, you should let me cut in front of you while you stand here and think about it." These types of students plagued the campus, both male and female. A true testament that identity crisis should be officially extended beyond the adolescent stage. One day as Lloyd and I sat in the cafeteria, a group of students struggled with their sexuality and tried to figure out whether they're gay or straight. One white girl told her friends, "You know what, by the end of the semester, if I sleep with more guys that means I'm strictly dickly. But If I end up sleeping with more girls then I'm all hers." Lloyd and I looked at each other then ran over to her table and began hanging out with the girl and her friends. Some students satisfied their urge and thirst for social status by joining a sorority and fraternity. Alpha Phi is a sisterhood of women supporting one another in lifelong achievement.

Delta Phi Epsilon was to provide a sisterhood experience with a rich tradition, innovation, and opportunities for growth. Zeta Phi Beta was to foster the ideas of service, charity, scholarship, civil and cultural endeavors, sisterhood, and finer womanhood. These ideals are reflected in the sorority's national program for which its members and auxiliary groups provide voluntary service to staff, community outreach programs, fund scholarships, support organized charities, and promote legislation for social and civic change. Sigma Gamma Rho was a woman's sorority whose aim is to enhance the quality of life within the community. Public Service, leadership development, and education of youth are the hallmark of the organization's programs and activities. Sigma Gamma Rho addresses concerns that impact society educationally, civically, and economically. That was the sorority that Vanessa joined. Lloyd and I had just finished playing basketball in the gym and sitting on the bleachers when she arrived looking incredibly sexy while sporting their trademark Royal Blue and Gold colors. "Hey boys, check out the newest sorority member." Lloyd joked, "Sweet, so how many guys did you have to blow in order to get into that club?" We laughed as she replied and showed a photo. "Actually, just one, the same guy that you also slept with Lloyd, oops did I spill the beans?" She walked away smiling, as I shockingly looked at Lloyd and asked "Hey man is that true?" He was embarrassed but quickly answered, "We were partying one night, I was so lit and it was no big deal. I totally forgot that it even happened." I burst out laughing, hahaha." But it really was no big deal because Lloyd was my friend and he had never crossed that line with me.

Omega Psi Phi was a men's fraternity that was founded on November 17th, 1911. They grant honorary memberships to men, who have contributed to society in a positive way. Alpha Delta

Gamma is a men's social fraternity that was founded on October 10th, 1924. It's based on Christian principles of true manhood, sound learning, and the unity of true manhood. Iota Phi Theta is a men's fraternity that was founded on September 19th, 1963 at Morgan State University. The all-black fraternity sought to eradicate segregation with a protest that was organized against the Northwood Shopping center in Hollywood. In 1992, the fraternity established the National Iota Foundation, a tax-exempt entity whose purpose is to assist the needy through scholarships and other financial assistance. Since its creation, the foundation has distributed over $250,000 in programs and services. They have a strong commitment to bringing about empowerment to the African American community. To join each of these fraternities and sororities each individual had to prove he, or she was worthy. For example, if the specific group drank a lot, then more than likely there would be some drinking involved with the requirements. Lloyd and I managed to get the secret location of one of these hazing incidents late one night and saw a guy chug so much beer he began vomiting profusely and was taken to the hospital for alcohol poisoning. During the winter, some guys sat out in the thirty-degree weather for a significant period of time with just a cardboard box covering their genitals. Meanwhile, across town at another university, a lawsuit was filed by a female student, who was trying to get into a sorority, provided excruciating details about how she was forced to stimulate sexual acts as well as engage in what could be considered as dangerous behavior. The plaintiff stated that she was forced to hold a plank position in the middle of the road during speeding traffic. She recalls being locked in a car until she drank a baby bottle filled with ketchup, hot sauce, mustard, and other kitchen items. According to the suit, she was forced to drink jello shots even after she informed her instructors that she was on medication and didn't want to drink. The claim went on to mention how the female student was forced to dress up like a male rapper, squat on top of another freshman, and stimulate sexual intercourse in front of the other members of the sorority.

Lastly, if not the most demoralizing, she was forced to read a letter in front of the sorority declaring her worthlessness. The student had become despondent and dropped out of school. I personally thought the fraternities were cool but I would have simply declined if I was ever issued such a requirement. However, these rituals are extremely similar to prison when wanting to join a gang. Some individuals join gangs in jail for protection, some were born in a gang or forced into a gang because of race or other affiliations. Similar to sororities in college, prospective members have to prove their loyalty by not inflicting pain on themselves but on other rival gangs or innocent people. It was on a very cold day when I had finally gotten off cell restriction. During my workout routine, I overheard a young Mexican guy talking to his friends and mentioned, "Man, I want to be down with the MS 13 homies, nobody can touch them, if you even think about it, they'll send one of the correctional officers to shoot up your house." The MS 13 is known to have about ten thousand members and it's one of the most dangerous and violent gangs in operation today. The gang was founded in the Salvadoran immigrant community of Los Angeles in the 1980s. They specialize in all types of illegal behavior; drug trafficking, murder, extortion, racketeering, and even child prostitution. The Aryan Brother Organization or the AB has a major stronghold on the federal penitentiary system in the United States. The AB is particularly a pretty scary group.

One major rule in order to join the gang is killing a black or Hispanic prisoner. Also, once you're in, you can't leave. You're in the brotherhood for life. They also have about ten thousand members. The notorious Blood Gang started in the 1960s in Los Angeles, and eventually spread to several prisons in Texas and spread to the East Coast in New York. Just last year, a judge sentenced one of the founders of the East Coast Bloods to 50 years in jail. The prosecutors proved that the East Coast Bloods Gang was the largest, violent street gang in New York City.

The Blood's well-known rivals are the Rollin 60 Crips, who have more than two thousand members recruited from the Westchester and Crenshaw neighborhoods of LA. They're known for their bank robberies, carjacking, deadly weapon assaults, and even rape. The Barrio Azteca is of heavy concern, not only local but international law enforcement has their eye on this group. With over several thousand members operating out of New Mexico, Texas, Massachusetts, and to my surprise my home State of Pennsylvania. The gang has been implicated in cocaine trafficking, high-profile murders, and even prison massacres. They're certainly not a crowd you want to be mingling with. In college, if one fraternity member had a problem with the other, no one was trying to stab or kill each other, they would have settled their differences with either a debate on a controversial topic or the most intense dance battle one could ever imagine. I stayed clear of all the garbage. I really think this is a complete joke and totally ashamed that people are that desperate to feel needed and would actually go to the extreme measures of hurting another person just to be accepted. It was during my tutoring of Nate, a young black guy, who was 19-years-old and had only one year remaining on his 10-year manslaughter sentence. He asked me to join him in a meeting later that evening with several of his friends. "Hey Nell, you want to hang out in the yard later? There's a meeting tonight, the most respected guys in the prison are going to be there." "I aggressively replied, "And you know what Nate, they're still going to be there when you and I are long gone. So no, I won't be attending the meeting tonight and neither should you."

The reason for my harsh reply was because Nate was a part of the Blood Gang. I've seen how he greeted other members with that funny handshake which was a dead giveaway that he might be gang affiliated. He replied, "Wow, no one here has ever spoken to me like that before." We were just a few years apart. I continued, "Look, you're a big boy now and at the end of the day, you're going to make your own decisions. But you've been incarcerated your entire teenage life. You missed some of the most pivotal, fun years of your life. Dude, you missed the prom and if you go back out there with the same garbage, you're going to miss the rest of what life has to offer." He was speechless as we began walking to the chow hall for dinner and he continued to be amazed. I told him about college, all the fun

I had, the girls, the parties, oh and the girls. He laughed; it was like telling a little kid a fairytale story. His face lit up when telling him about all the concerts I went to. "I saw Snoop Dogg, Chris Brown, and Rihanna in concert." "Wow, but I could never go to college, that work would be too damn hard for me bro." "Hmm. look at it this way, if you were to somehow make it playing football in the NFL, do you think you'd be playing against a junior high school team?" He answered "No, but I get your point. The work is supposed to be hard because that's the level you're on."

Just because he was studying for his G.E.D and failed to envision himself being on a prestigious campus. I saw great potential in Nate. He kind of reminded me of Kenny, who was still on the run. I had a few options of where he could be but as time passed my anger dissolved and I held no grudge against Kenny. I actually wished him well. It was the additional time that I spent in the study room with Nate that brought peace to my heart about Kenny. Nate began to read educational books, his vocabulary vastly increased while his participation in gang activities diminished. On a sunny afternoon, as we sat in the study room, three of his fellow gang members confronted us. One who went by the name of Fats expressed concern. "Yo blood, what's up with you? You haven't been to any of the meetings lately. You know the others were asking for you and thought that you were trying to leave." Nate scarcely replied, "Naw man, I just been here on a different vibe. Cornell really got me on another way of thinking." I just sat there with a smirk on my face as Fats, and his friends stared at me then Fats angrily replied, this tutor has been feeding you a bunch of garbage. There's a meeting tonight after chow, you better be there," "But I have studying to do," Nate uttered, but Fats and his friends didn't even respond, they just walked out of the room. To keep the peace, I told Nate to, "Go to the meeting, but just meet me back here tomorrow after chow." "Ok." Later that evening, Nate went to the meeting and was chastised by the Bloods leader named Suggs. The Suge Knight reject stated, "So, you've been M.I.A for the last couple of weeks." Nate replied, "Suggs it's all good, I just been trying to get a lot of studying done." "Yes, I've heard, that seems to be the case with you and about a dozen others. All this talk about college, leaving the gang, your family, your brotherhood, and who the hell is this Cornell Richards anyway?" "Fats answered, it's the new tutor in the study room." Suggs then stated, "Tutor huh? Well, it seems like I'm going to have to teach this tutor a lesson about messing with my family." The next day I hadn't seen Nate all day. I thought maybe he was just tired and would meet me later after chow. That evening, dinner was actually pretty good. The chicken dinner and vegetables gave me a little taste of home.

There were poll lights along the walkway but it was still a little dark. There was usually a C.O in the booths along the path but maybe they had other business to attend to or had taken their lunch break. But as I walked towards my housing unit, I was ambushed by four Blood Gang members. One big guy just stood by and watched, it had to be Suggs. I'm confident that I broke one of the guy's jaws, as he fell in the bushes but the other two guys tossed me on the ground and began kicking and punching me in the stomach. I guarded my face as they repeatedly beat me. I then saw a sharp blade but one person said, "No, you don't have to do that. Let's go." Then I heard their footsteps take off in the dark. The voice belonged to Nate. Seconds later, I vomited my entire meal and immediately knew that he was under a certain amount of pressure to prove his loyalty, and I was more grateful that things didn't go too far. Of course, the idiot C.O finally arrived and asked me, "Hey are you alright?" I just said, "Yeah, I'm just not feeling well but I'm cool." The next few days, my ribs and back were completely sore but I was still in the study room because others needed my help. Nate entered the room and sat next to me. I said, "You better get away from me because they might do you next or worse." "Look Nell, I wasn't going to let them do that to you. I'm out man, seriously I'm out." "So, what now, you'll take protective custody? If not, you'll be a moving target." "Hell no, I'll just switch the housing units. Bloods stick together and there's none in the mid-section of the jail, so that means I can still see you during the regular times for tutoring." "Ok cool, sounds like a plan." I was the tutor but Nate's decision to finally leave the gang was inspirational and

I was excited that my sessions with him hadn't ended. He had a tremendously bright future and this clown Suggs was acting like an obsessive, controlling lunatic. It took exactly one week for Nate to get his housing unit switched and we resumed his studies. My popularity had grown throughout the jail with the leading rumor being that I made studying for the G.E.D test simply much easier and the number of passing inmates had increased by 30% from the previous year.

CHAPTER 4

Ferocity

I'VE ALWAYS WANTED to go away to college but the out-of-state tuition forced me to remain local. By the grace of God, I never experienced any school shootings. One of my options for out-of-state studying was Virginia Tech but they sent me a nice, little rejection letter in the mail. It was clear that God's rejection was for my protection. I was supposed to attend a field trip during my senior year in high school the same day when the Virginia Tech massacre took place in April of 2007. Glad I followed my instincts because something told me to keep my ass home. A student shot and killed thirty-two people and wounded seventeen others in two separate attacks. Another six people were injured, trying to escape through classroom windows. This attack is the second deadliest shooting incident by a single gunman in U.S History. Surpassed only by an Orlando nightclub shooting in 2016 which was certainly one of the deadliest by a single gunman in the world. The shooting at Northern Arizona University in 2015 which killed one and injured three was the 52nd shooting on school grounds that year and the 23rd on a college campus according to a group that advocates for gun reform. The epidemic continued with a shooter at the University of Maryland, who fatally shot himself and his roommate, and had a history of mental illness. That same year in June a shooting rampage at Santa

Monica College in California left five people dead, including the gunman. At the Stevens Institute of Business & Arts in St. Louis, a student allegedly shot an administrator during a financial aid dispute. The University of Washington D.C wasn't spared, as one student was shot and killed in a random robbery attempt. Unbelievably, I had also applied for graduate school at all of these schools and received a rejection letter. Another common act of violence on college campuses is the concern number of allegations regarding a sexual assault with 2011 being the most popular. In 2014 there were twelve reported rapes. A 2019 Association of American Universities survey on sexual assault and misconduct polled over 150,000 students at 27 universities. One could easily make the argument that a prison campus is safer than a college campus. You are greeted by metal detectors as soon as you step foot on a prison campus, opposed to a college campus where anyone can simply enter the grounds without proper identification. Only the school's learning labs, libraries, or computer labs are secured. Generally, anyone can roam free with the luxury of disguising themselves by simply wearing the university's t-shirt.

Of course, there were fights in the penitentiary, with one being the most gruesome when a younger white guy beat the crap out of an older black guy. The two-minute skirmish was over a pack of cigarettes but left a lasting blood trail. There were occasional assaults on staff. Sporadically, more so comical, you even had staff members, assaulting other staff members due to obvious frustration from heavy caseloads. Besides, being jumped that night by Suggs's attack dogs, there was no rioting, no jailbreaks, or gang rapes that I observed during my unexpected vacation. The case of someone being raped in that facility was very, less likely to happen. The jail superiors controlled the facility by having a specific unit for those, who openly admitted to being gay at the time of the intake process where all health and personal questions are asked such as your sexual preference. This of course doesn't necessarily eliminate but it minimizes chaos and allows homosexuality to be more invited than forced. The environment was more so of a therapeutic community. I had now completed Mr. Phelps's classes. There were more days than I actually enjoyed waking up and seeing the breathtaking mountain views and welcomed the fresh, brisk air. The beautiful sunset indicated one day closer to home which some days were discouraging. Honestly, the milieu looked better than most places in my West Philadelphia neighborhood that had disgracefully earned the nickname "West Philthy" because of the grimy streets. One night, Stanley ranted after having a dull day, "I'm really pissed about being here. Rapists and murderers get off every day. I should have put in that appeal." I then intended to cheer him up, "Far as I'm concerned, this is a freaking vacation. Free heat, free weight room with no membership fee, free food, free laundry, free television. All courtesy of taxpayer's hard-earned dollars. Not a care in the world for our actions, so we're good." He laughed as my insensitivity was meant to keep him in high spirits.

The next day I worked out in the yard, continuing to chisel my slender frame. I noticed a white and a black guy sitting at a table staring at me, I ignored them. I also noticed a few members of the Bloods staring at me but I ignored them as well. The white guy then walked over to me and asked, "Hey, did you just recently graduate from college?" Surprised, I answered "Yes." "Damn, I knew it by the way that you carried yourself. Oh, I'm Ryan Dillard, Delta Gamma." I was familiar with their handshake and we greeted each other. "Hey Ryan, I'm Cornell Richards, nice to meet you under the circumstances." Right after we greeted each other, we were hostilely approached by two Bloods. One asked, "Yo homie, what set y'all claiming?" The black guy that Ryan was sitting with quickly ran over and explained, "No, no, no, they're not in a gang. They went to college, they're in a fraternity." Confused, the Blood member asked, "What the hell is a fraternity?" Ryan humorously elucidated, "Well it's almost like a gang but it's a group of men that focuses on Christian principles of true brotherhood and manhood." The other gang member seemed intrigued but they both simply just walked away. I then thanked Ryan's friend, "Thanks for intervening," He replied, "It's sad how ignorance can be so condemning. I'm Justin," "Nice meeting you Justin, did you attend our university as well?"

No, I was rejected, I graduated from another college with a degree in English. I made some poor decisions and got hit with a drug charge." I just shook my head as Ryan explained his situation, "Yeah, the tuition payment got pretty rough for me after graduation and I got hit for money laundering. The tuition was paid, now I'm paying." "Gotcha." Shockingly, Ryan then said, "We heard what happened to you. Several of my friends were at the party that night and also got their lockers checked." I replied, "Yeah, it's cool, things happen for a reason." They were from the same housing unit as Nate. It was now time to return and assured each other we'd link up again soon. That night, as I laid in bed and reflected on my interesting day. All of the inspiration that I received from Nate, even the beating from Suggs's crew, had contributed to what was boiling inside of me in an attempt to set a trend and establish greatness. As stated in the previous chapter the fraternities and sororities in college each had a specific mission and the gangs in prison were also well-known for particular crimes. Realistically, I had my doubts but the energy was too strong. I had plans to start my own gang/ fraternity at Coal Township. When mentioning it to Stanley, he lashed out, "Man you're delusional, you're getting way too carried away with this save the world crap. Just chill out and mind your own damn business, and don't draw any attention to our cell. I have a release date and I don't need any drama."

Maybe he was right. Maybe I was overreacting and not thinking clearly. My life could be in danger and my body shipped to my noted address. But I felt it, this was a movement, and the next day as it poured down raining, there was no tutoring to conduct, so myself, Ryan, Justin, and Nate huddled up at a table in the study room and I told them the plan. "Let's specialize in recruiting current gang members and making them into college students by offering free prep courses." Ryan replied, "So what do we do, hand out flyers?" Nate laughed but Justin said, "I'm on board, I'm just curious how we spread the word. I answered, it's simple, we plant the seed and watch it grow. Nate although you said you were out; it would actually make more sense if you stayed in with the Bloods. I could use you as a decoy." He answered, "Ok cool, I could just tell them that I was forced to move to another unit in order to make more room for other offenders." "Nice," I replied. Nate then asked, "So what will I be saying?" "You won't have to say much; your actions will speak louder than your words. But simply spread the word that college sessions are free in the study lab. I'm going to have my mom send all of my books from college. My shipment will look like a miniature library." Ryan agreed, "Genius, I will have my folks do the same, so we'll have double the material." I was thrilled but explained, "Excellent but this is only for inmates, who pass the G.E.D test. So hopefully this incentive will motivate more inmates to want to take the test." Nate then added, "I'll have my folks send my books to triple that notion but what do we call ourselves?" I shook my head in agreement then answered "Nothing fancy, but it makes sense. Frat Gang." Ryan replied, "I love it." He then looked at Nate and said, "Kid get started." But we were all kids with me being the oldest at 23 years old. I got Ms. Foley's blessings after explaining my scheme. "Sure, go ahead Cornell and I'll back you." Word quickly spread around the entire prison about the new free college prep courses that we would be conducting. Every chance he got Nate returned back with info of those more curious to leave the Bloods Gang and join us but was of course afraid for their lives. We made a bold statement by all four of us always being together when eating during chow time, and in the yard since those were the major platforms to showcase that we should be taken seriously.

Mother sent the books about two weeks later, and I just told her that I would be simply donating them. The fifty-book package certainly drew attention from other inmates, when my name was called for mail. Stanley just stood by his bed, watching me like a hawk, as I checked to make sure that my entire order was fulfilled. Ryan's order also arrived with his delivery being exactly the same size followed by Nate's parcel arriving a few days later. We could feel the tension from gang leaders as the flood gates opened and we recruited member after member. Members from the MS 13, The Aryan Brother Organization, Bloods Gang. The Blood's well-known rivals, the Rollin 60 Crips, and The Barrio Azteca. When they came to our study room, we all were unified. Ryan issued the mission statement. "Regardless of our different social backgrounds and race we're all here to achieve the same goal and that's to accomplish a prestigious education. That's the brotherhood when you join Frat Gang. You have to be 115% committed, if not you're wasting your time." Everyone was on board and within a month we had about three hundred members. Ryan and I both consolidated our G.E.D tutoring and our college prep tutoring, so we could do more damage. Stanley began to indirectly have a change of heart as I caught him enjoying one of my books that I purposely left behind to keep my memory fresh. After being caught red-handed he amusingly just threw it back on the table. Mr. Phelps, the instructor, stopped me one day in the hallway and said, "Wow Richards, you're doing a better job than the people that actually work here." I humbly replied, "Thank you, sir, it's all because of my great team and the people believing in change." "Listen to you, your team? Have a good one Richards." It was a rewarding day but an exhausting one as well. A quick shower and a snack were the only two things that were needed to put me out like a light. But around 2 am in the morning someone kicked my door very loudly and slid a note under the door. Terrified, Stanley and I both jumped up but the person had disappeared.

It could have been a C.O, or an overnight inmate worker who was cleaning. I grabbed the note as Stanley hit the light switch. The letter read, "DEAD COON ASS NIGGERS." Stanley then began to freak out. "See, I told you not to start this crap, now these idiots are sending death threats here, and to the best of my knowledge, if they can't get you, they'll get me because I'm your celly." I was highly concerned but played it cool and nonchalantly told him, "Man, this is a bunch of garbage, just go back to bed." The very next morning on the way to the study room, I saw a crowd of inmates and paramedics, surrounding another inmate laying on the ground. It was Nate. He was stabbed several times by some unknown gang members. I turned around and saw Suggs staring at me, I didn't know if he was responsible but I dropped my books and before I could go after him, his bodyguards surrounded him. Ryan grabbed me and said,

"Cornell don't do it, we came too far. This is not the way." I sat on the ground crying hoping Nate would move but I saw the paramedics cover him with the white blanket. The jail was on lockdown for the next several days, until investigators could find out which gang members killed him. Meanwhile, as I suffered in self-blame and was momentarily an outcast because of the other inmates' restriction of watching television and playing board games, my door buzzed and a young, white male C.O appeared. He barked, "Richards get dressed now, the warden wants to see you." I was shocked. Stanley and I just looked at each other, rightfully curious as the C.O guarded the door. Stanley said, "Man this just keeps getting better, people are getting killed, now you're in hot water with the warden."

While getting dressed in my cleanest attire, a feeling of excitement emerged. Two correctional officers along with a huge German Shepherd then escorted me through the unit, and I looked back and could see the inmates gawking with curiosity through their doors. When reaching the administration building, the officer that knocked on my door then politely asked, "Richards do you need to use the bathroom before your meeting with the warden?" "Ahh.. yeah," I quickly used the restroom and returned with the officer telling me to enter the warden's office. Still nervous but excited, both officers entered the room behind me and stood by the door with the dog, ready to attack on command. I then saw a drop-dead gorgeous goddess, with a dominating presence quickly approaching, and extending her palm to shake my hand. "Cornell Richards, it's finally nice to meet you. I'm Warden Green." "Nice to meet you, warden." "Please, sit down young man." She was Caucasian, tall with gray eyes and wearing a tight ashen, power suit and favored the great, Carla Gugino. Even the dog was blushing. I sat in front of her desk as she continued, "First let me say that I'm terribly sorry about what happened to your friend, it was also brought to my attention all of the great things you've managed to accomplish so far, during your first year here at Coal Township. But I have to be honest Mr. Richards, there has been enough bloodshed, don't you think you should close down your operation?" Ha! I scorched the beautiful demon. "My operation? Warden your facility is overcrowded by one thousand inmates, you're in violation by not having proper sleeping quarters for inmates and issuing them mattresses to sleep on in an old gym room. The only thing that needs to be closed down ma'am, is this facility and freeing the oppressed." With her face boiling hot, she looked up at the officers and requested for them to, "Leave us."

One officer hesitated, "But warden," she then demanded, "Leave us now." When they left the room, she walked around the desk and we were face to face. She was breathtaking, even during her insults. "I've seen your record; no prior convictions and I know that you got screwed by the system. But you're in my hands now, pretty boy, and if you think you got screwed once, try me Cornell, and I'll make sure that you leave this place limb by limb. You're a criminal, just like the rest of them." I almost crapped in my pants but if that was the case, I was pretty much already dead. Before replying I thought about Lloyd, I thought about Nate, and what they would want. I could hear them both clearly telling me to set her straight. A tear-drop ran down my face before verbally hurling my brimstones. "You would rather keep the inmates suppressed and ignorant while your bank account increases. I've managed to recruit over three hundred gang members for a tremendous cause, and if anything happens to me, they'll turn sour and that would probably interrupt your little sun tanning sessions. Good day to you, Warden Green." When I walked out and slammed the door, she yelled, "You son of a bitch." Coincidentally, someone was playing the radio loudly and Kanye West's legendary verse mentioned, "The prettiest people do the ugliest things, for the road to riches and diamond rings." The officers escorted me back to my unit. Stanley apparently applied for a transfer earlier in the week to another cell as he moved out when the facility reopened and I was without a cellmate. Cool! Word quickly spread about my secret meeting with the warden. Overall, violence decreased but because of my new fraternity, a few of my members were beaten up by some correctional officers but we were destined to persevere. It gave us a taste of the civil rights movement because we stood up for what we believed in and stood up for people who couldn't defend themselves.

Assaults from the correctional officers continued to mount. We were then placed in solitary confinement. The phones were intentionally damaged, so our phone calls to our family members were depleted. During visiting hours, the disrespect towards our families had become intolerable. What was supposed to be a regularly scheduled family visit, an officer told the mother of one of my fraternity brothers to, "Hurry up so we can search you or don't come back." My fraternity brother lost his temper and punched the officer, my frat brother was then beaten and dragged out in front of his baby daughter as she screamed for her daddy. Our full course meals had been reduced to a portion more fitting for a toddler. When we ordered our commissary, the orders were not completed. Our colored uniforms returned with bleach stains and our whites returned with brown stains. The correctional officers intentionally strolled past our unit whenever handing out the sign-up sheets for the barbershop. When sick call arrived, the nurses took their grand old time. Several of my guys had asthma and needed their prescriptions refilled immediately. The plague that the warden had obviously unleashed for me not submitting, had actually started to take its toll on us. Her evil deeds continued as our 40-inch flat-screen on the unit was disconnected. How wonderful that the cleaning supplies were minimized and the heat was turned down in the middle of the winter. It gets even better, well at least for the few of my guys, who had their conjugal visits revoked. Whenever we issued grievances, they were basically ignored. That's when members of my fraternity expressed their frustration towards me. One white guy said, "Look, I really think we should throw in the towel." Others yelled, "Yeah Cornell, we can't live like this." I knew that it was obviously a tactic from the warden to get us to break, but it was a bit more difficult to get the others to understand, especially those who were affected and were not a part of my fraternity. They were hot with me.

During this time, I was looking like a mad man because I haven't had a haircut in a couple of months. So, I took another chance with the razor and trimmed my hair. I immediately disposed of it by tossing it in a trash can outside the unit. I momentarily lost the confidence of the fraternity but my immediate captains remained hopeful. Ryan stated, "Look since the warden wants to play hardball, we have to turn up the heat on her as well." Justin agreed while rubbing his hands together because of the cold as we contemplated our new scheme in the yard. "Yeah, anything to get the fraternity back in good standings." I didn't want to provide false hope and become egotistical so I bravely admitted, "Look, we accomplished a lot but we need help." Ryan asked, "So what do you have in mind?" "I'm going to first ask Ms. Foley to print out all the times the warden made a request to see the list in our study room because that's how the warden knows who to screw over. Then I'll request to see Mr. Phelps, the violence prevention instructor. I'll ask him just to simply observe the cutbacks that have been going on around the jail and why all of a sudden there are more inmates going into solitary confinement. Those inmates are our fraternity brothers. With less enthusiasm, I mentioned, "If that doesn't work then I'll request to see the warden and apologize to her. We can't have the entire jail suffer because of our struggle. Alright, get some sleep tonight gentlemen, we'll meet tomorrow in the study room." The very next day as Ryan and Justin did some tutoring, I explained everything to Ms. Foley. She replied "Oh, that woman needs to get laid, she's such a complete bitch. But here's what I can do for you Cornell, first I'm going to pretend that you and I never had this conversation because I would be fired. I'll then print out some information and place it over there on my desk, so just in case you get caught it will look like you stole it. So, whatever you choose to do is your business. Good Luck"

I immediately got flashbacks of seeing myself on the camera in the courtroom placing Kenny's hoodie in my locker. Minutes later, I saw when Ms. Foley placed the papers on her desk. When class was over, I attempted to go over and quickly snatch them but an inmate walked by and accidentally knocked them on the floor. He thought they were mine and apologized while gathering the papers and simply placed them in my hand. I knew Ms. Foley was watching so I just turned around and we smirked at each other. Ryan and Justin met me in the hallway. I confirmed, "One down, one to go," while showing them the documents. It was lunchtime and I knew that Phelps would be walking to the cafeteria, so I stalled by going to the bathroom as his class was just finishing up. Right on time, the inmates were heading out but I noticed Phelps still seated at his desk and not preparing to exit the classroom. Quick thinking, I asked the C.O who at the time was monitoring the hallway, "Hey, sorry to bother you but I left some study material in that classroom, can I go back and get them?" He rudely answered, "Make it fast." Phelps was glad to see me. "Hey, kid." I quickly explained, and Phelps agreed but stated "You know what you've gotta do to make your agenda more significant?" "Sure what?" "You're good with words Richards, so utilize that skill, instead of hammering back at the warden, issue a proposal to the state. Cornell, you've got a college degree, thanks to you about half of these guys can now spell college. You don't need my, or anyone else's confirmation because you're the prisoner. But of course, I see the crappy food they're serving down at the cafeteria, why do you think I'm sitting here with my brown paper bag and freezing my nuts off in here. If the state asks me any questions, I'll back you." Wow, this was huge, I thanked Phelps for thoroughly advising me and also the C.O in the hallway as I quickly returned to the unit.

CHAPTER 5

Statement

MR. PHELPS HAD given me some great advice but that advice gave me PTSD (Post-Traumatic Stress Disorder). The last time I wrote a proposal was during my sophomore year in college after being placed on Academic Probation for the second time. Although this matter concerned a small group of students who were struggling tremendously, everyone deserves a fair shot. So, I wrote a proposal intending to ban academic probation. In my policy, I first mentioned the school's condemning restrictions. "Any student who showed a history of failure was placed on academic probation and had to sit out for the entire four-month semester and was not allowed to enter school grounds. Due to the student's grade point average falling below 2.0, the student would still have to remain financially responsible for the courses he or she initially registered for. The student also loses financial aid because of the obvious poor performance. When the semester ends, the student can re-register for courses but remains financially responsible for the courses he or she is pursuing until the GPA reaches a 2.0 then the student can re-apply for financial aid." I was in the library and was interrupted by Vanessa when getting started on the proposal. "Hey, whatcha doing?" "Hey trouble, I decided to write a proposal to ban academic probation." She jokingly replied, "Ah, I see they struck a nerve and finally got you to do some work." "Very funny but I just don't understand, why should a student be kicked out of school because they're struggling?" "Hmm..well how about those students find the same energy that got them here in the first place. But I guess those slackers can depend on people like you to bail them out. Your little proposal is certainly going to lower the standards of the school Cornell Richards, shame on you." She then walked away.

Maybe she had a point. That's what I really liked about Vanessa, she challenged me, never afraid to voice her opinion but more importantly, she was making me a better individual. But this proposal was meant for something positive and most of all, I would rather the department heads turn me down than not issue the proposal at all. My objective simply stated that my intent was to help the small number of students that fell in this category. Instead of discontinuing the student's studies for an entire semester, the psychological impact could be extremely detrimental resulting in the student not returning to the university. Allow the student to take only one class but the student will be held financially responsible for the course. This will be exceedingly beneficial for the student because he or she will still have access to the facility to use the computer labs, math labs, science labs, etc. As opposed to the current policy that implies the student not being allowed on the campus. In most cases, the university is unclear about why the student is struggling, so it makes more sense to have that student around a positive, influential setting as opposed to a possibly hostile environment that many students may be experiencing in their personal lives. Once the student demonstrates a history/ reaching a grade point average of 2.0. the student can apply for financial aid to take more classes because the government only provides aid to students taking two or more classes as the current policy stated. I concluded similarly to my objective that the motive was to simply have the student's studies be continued by providing a new alternative. Before submitting the proposal, Lloyd took a look as I relaxed in his dorm room. He said, "Nell this is actually pretty good. But damn, you gotta be a complete screw-up to fall below a 2.0. What's your G.P.A now? "I'm at 1.90." "Holy crap, what have you been doing, going to class with your freaking eyes closed?" "I dropped a couple of courses and failed a few. Thank goodness for Ms. Carol, Vanessa's aunt, she's still allowing me to work, so I can pay the rent." "Lucky son of a gun." When I finally submitted the proposal to the Director of Student Affairs, the mid-age Hispanic beauty skimmed through it, then provided her thoughts. "You know what Mr. Richards, your proposal is very pretty but this is one of the best universities in the country and if students can't get their crap together, especially after being dropped more than twice such as yourself then they don't deserve to be here. So no, this proposal is DENIED, good luck this semester." I walked out of her office, balled up the proposal, and just threw it in the trash can. That semester I received C's in all three of my courses and was in good standings. The reason why I was still able to graduate within four years is because I took extra classes in the summer at the local community college. One thing that motivated me to write a good proposal for our fraternity while in prison was remembering what Vanessa said about students finding the energy that got them to college in the first place. So, on a rainy day, I sat in my cell and meticulously wrote a proposal exposing the warden for her tyranny against my fraternity brothers and others throughout the facility. My door buzzed and Officer Benson and another white correctional officer briefly interrupted me. Benson asked, "So what are you up to now Richards?" I kept it short and sweet. "Oh, nothing much, just a little artwork." The other officer then replied, "You're so full of shit." Then they slammed the door. Before submitting the proposal, I respectively gave copies to both Ryan and Justin to review, with them in return, giving me the go-ahead.

"Yup, sounds good to me." "Yup, send it." I didn't trust putting the proposal in the mail, so I asked Phelps to do the honors and send it off to the State. He was obliged, "Gotcha, I'll send it priority mail and have them sign for it." "Ok cool. Thank you kind sir." About two weeks went by and it was like a flip of the switch. The harassment from officers had ceased, our meals were twice the average size, and the heat was properly adjusted. The medications were being handed out on time, the phones were working, and my fraternity brothers enjoyed their visits with their family members. Over the next few weeks, we saw a new class of correctional officers that were hired and the new recruits did their job with a smile. Most of all the television was reconnected and slightly enhanced with the new high-definition feature. There was a memo issued to every prisoner in the jail, apologizing for the inconvenience and justifying the inhumane treatment with a fancy lie described as "Technical Difficulties and Brief Shortage of Supplies." Whenever I walked through the campus, the correctional officers greeted me by name. "Good morning Mr. Richards, good afternoon Mr. Richards, Have a goodnight, Mr. Richards." Phelps was amazed, and admitted, "Now honestly, I was tempted to open the proposal and read it, but my God, actions speak louder than words. You must have written some heat. These people are treating you like a damn rock star. I mean, I've been working here for seventeen years, and I don't get treated like a rock star." I couldn't help but laugh and thanked him for strongly advising me. "Thanks again, I really appreciate the support." I went to see Ms. Foley to thank her for the little role she played in our success as she was overwhelmed with joy and threw herself at me, giving me a hug once I entered the study room. "You are truly something special Cornell Richards. Thank you for putting your pen where your mouth is." I wasn't arrogant but did enjoy the fame and special treatment. I was getting extra warm blankets and my laundry was being done two or three times a week. I was blessed with additional time in the study room. Some officers brought in gourmet sandwiches, hot soups, and Starbucks coffee for my captains, as I made it clear that my preference was peach herbal tea.

Occasionally, when in the mood for sports, I would watch some television with the guys, who thankfully welcomed me back into their good graces. But one morning as I sat in my cell sipping my peach tea from my executive decision mug, my door buzzed with two officers holding a gigantic box and mentioning "Mr. Richards, special delivery." It felt like Christmas as I invited them inside to help me open the 65-inch television. It was almost twice the size of the television for our one-hundred-man unit. The TV almost covered the entire wall in my 9x12 cell. The harassment then began about folks wanting to be my new cellmate. Of course, all personal inquiries were denied and I made it clear to the officers that I didn't want anyone moving in with me. Since that request was an understandable issue because they needed the extra bed to provide proper sleeping quarters. I was given three options by my soft-spoken, white, mid-age unit counselor Mr. Smith. "Cornell, you've got three options. A. Choose a respectable roommate. B. Move into a dormitory or C. Move across the campus where the remaining one-man cells are but they're infested with Bloods Gang members. I answered, "I'm geared towards C. That's how much I really don't want to live with anyone." Smith instructed, "But with that move, you probably wouldn't be living at all, they would tear you apart, especially with your new-found lifestyle." "Point taken." Smith then gave me a solution. "I'll give you a list of twenty inmates, none of whom match your qualifications and mannerism but civil and who are nonviolent offenders. Scope them out and make your final decision in a week. I'm under the gun here to fill that space." "Ok understandable." Smith had a job to do, so that was fair. When I left the office, a loudmouth guy named Gus offered me a proposal. He was clearly eavesdropping on our conversation.

"Step into my office," he boasted. I've never spoken to him before because of his tough-guy routine. He often walked around the unit with his shirt off attempting to intimidate others with his upper masculine frame but his skinny chicken legs said otherwise. Anyway, I briefly stood by his cell which was the only one-man room on the unit. He then offered, "How about you trade me your television for my cell? I noticed that you're never on the unit and I have a 30-year sentence. You'll be gone in a couple of years, so this is a good offer, you get your sanity without putting your life in danger by moving over there with those idiots and I get to burn time with tons of entertainment. I'm also cool with Smith and can make this happen right now. So, what do you say Cornell?" Just by him mentioning my name in that con artist tone, gave me chills. This was a scary dude.

I quickly answered, "I'll get back to you." Then I quickly walked away. After a couple of hours of contemplating, I said to myself, "Hell no. I'm keeping my TV. It was my trophy from whoever sent it for all of my hard work. There are some people in society that can't even afford a 65-inch television and I got one in prison for free. I wasn't sent to jail to make this clown's sentence any easier. Maybe his 30-year sentence was a gift rather than a lethal injection. I really couldn't stand this guy, the nerve of him offering me a proposal. I decided to pick one of the candidates from Smith's list after he slid it under my door. Dexter, a black guy in his mid-thirties was selected. He was from another unit. I've seen him a few times in the library and also overheard him speak about how black people need to be more unified.

Did I make the wrong perception? He moved in the next day and introduced himself, "Hey I'm Dexter, wow it's like a mansion in here. I smirked, then introduced myself as well. "I'm Cornell, thanks." He then talked my head off for the next two hours. "Man, this place is crazy, these dudes in here are something else. I've been locked up for the past several years and been in about hmm... thirteen fights." Smith must have made a mistake by putting this idiot on the list. Thirteen fights? Dexter was clearly a violent person. His mouth continued to run like a chainsaw, so I tried to weather the storm by offering him something to eat, so he could shut the hell up. "Hey, would you like some soup or some chips?" "No, why am I talking too much?" I didn't want to be rude and say, yes and create bad vibes. "No, you're cool." He changed his mind, "A matter of fact, yeah I'll take a cup of soup from you." I gave him a cup of soup with an extra-large honey bun. It worked for a while, I had to check myself because maybe I was being too harsh and maybe Dexter was just excited to be my roommate as he acknowledged my popularity. "You are the man, I heard about you getting all of these free things and how the officers have been treating you and your team. I never believed anything in jail, but now I see for myself." "Thanks, yeah I'm glad things are back to normal." Weeks went by and one afternoon as I laid down, reading the newspaper, Dexter finally built up the confidence to disclose, "Hey Cornell, I hope you don't look at me any different but I once took a sex offender's class." "No Dex, I really could care less. I'm not that type of person." "I know, that's why I felt comfortable telling you."

He continued, "It was my first case, at 19 years old. I lived in Norristown, Pa and this chick just kept on playing around being indecisive about having intercourse. She called me around 1 am in the morning and was wearing booty shorts and a t-shirt. She kept on laughing saying, no stop, no stop, and I just ripped those things off and took the kitty but they only gave me three years." I just shook my head and chuckled as he continued. "The crazy thing is during the class; this one guy told the group how he sexually molested a baby. He said that he had to split the baby open so he could go inside the baby." I actually felt my stomach turn and just shook my head. His stories were disturbing but it's clear that he was perhaps still traumatized and struggling with some demons and needed to vent. He then asked about joining my fraternity which I knew would be his next question. "Hey man, I'm definitely trying to get on your team." This would not be a good idea, because I would now be seeing him even more during study time and living with him. I mean, who really wants to bring their work home with them? Regardless of his annoyance, a disservice would have been done on my end, if I kept info from him. So, I assigned him to Justin's list and he immediately began studying for his G.E.D. Nature began to take its place as I was now becoming sexually frustrated. Receiving gratification on a daily basis was the norm and it's been a year and a half since the graduation party. Fondling myself was typical but a full-length marathon of masturbating was totally out of the question, especially with Dexter's inconveniencing presence. Then the unimaginable happened. My door buzzed at 2 am in the morning, Dexter was knocked out and didn't even hear when Officer Rome, a young, white, C.O whispered, "Richards the warden wants to see you." Of course, I replied, "What? But it's two in the morning." "Hey, I'm just the messenger but get dressed." I had just woken up but the officer was the one with the stinky morning breath.

CHAPTER 6

I'm the man

I CERTAINLY WASN'T up for any drama and truthfully, I was more scared than the first time I met with this witch. This time only Officer Rome escorted me to the administration building and he didn't have the dog. We walked down the campus like two college buddies going to class. I asked him, "Do you have any idea what this is about?" "Nope, just following orders but you can walk straight into the office." This was truly bizarre. I entered the room as instructed and saw the tyrant sitting by the huge glass window, staring at the pale moonlight. I asked her, "What's this about?" She was pleasantly calm, "Oh relax, did I wake you from your little beauty sleep?" "I'm usually a night owl but it's been a long day," I replied. "You think you're so cute." She left the window and walked closer towards me until we were once again standing face to face. She admitted, "I read your little proposal, using all those fancy words. I have to admit, it turned me on." I looked at her awkwardly, while thinking, "This chick is more super crazy than I initially thought. I basically tried to have her fired by the State." I asked, "Are you serious?" She was convincing, "But more importantly, I'm glad that you're enjoying the television that I sent you. You got everything you wanted from the State." She then grabbed me by the collar. "Now give me what I want." I was completely surprised. It couldn't have been a trap because the most important question would have been, "What the hell was I doing in the warden's office at 2 am anyway?" She then slipped a condom into my palm. She slowly removed her heels and wrapped her leg around my calf muscle and aggressively began to unbutton my shirt. I tossed her onto the desk, her tongue tasted of cinnamon but I ripped off her panties. Her vagina was more savoring and was recently cleaned with some sort of tropical body wash.

We moved to the love seat, near the glass window and I began thrusting her from the back as she stuffed my shirt in her mouth to lower the sounds of her moaning. I used my shirt like a rein and rode her like a thoroughbred, gunning for the triple crown. She then allowed me to relax and gulped my entire manhood. We ended the session with her riding me and us climaxing at the same time. The full moonlight revived the room. Exhausted, but still in disbelief that we're now cuddling as her head rested on my chest. I asked, "I thought I was just a criminal?" She jokingly replied, "You are, now get the hell out before I set the dogs on you and call rape." We both laughed, then she asked "Are you thirsty?" We drank some orange juice, I then asked "Hey, so what about Officer Rome?" She got up, checked the camera, and said, "This slacker is outside of my door sleeping. But I'm glad that I chose him and not one of the other idiots who take their job too seriously." I just sat there, still in disbelief of what just happened, and even pinched myself twice to make sure that I wasn't dreaming. She saw me, "No, Cornell you're not dreaming, so stop pinching yourself." I smirked then took the last sip of my orange juice. Her performance was incredible. I admired her humor, a totally different person than the vicious creature I first met. She then asked while smiling and placing emphasis, "So if you're not too busy and you HAVE TIME, would you like to see me again?" "I'll be around," "Haha. I know where to find you and here's some more orange juice." She gave me a kiss as I went out the door. I then woke up Rome who was still sleeping by kicking his chair. "Hey, time to get up." Frightened and confused he gathered himself and said, "Oh, ok Mr. Richards, no problem." I went back to my cell and slept all day like a baby.

The last time I had a similar encounter was during my sophomore year in college. I was roaming the halls like it was high school and saw the college Dean, talking on the phone in her office. Her name was Celeste. She was African American, beautiful, mid-age, with shoulder-length hair with gray streaks. She was sophisticatedly dressed for her position and was well-spoken but I interrupted her conversation and cleverly pretended to be lost. When I approached the threshold, she provided me with great customer service and rushed the other person off the phone. "Ok there's a student in my office, I'll call you back. Hello young man, how can I help you?" I replied with a devilish grin, "I've seemed to have lost my way, I'm looking for your heart." She laughed, then admitted, "Ok that was cute." I moved aggressively, "Are you married?" "Huh no, I'm divorced but I'm not going to have this conversation with you now, here's my card, you can call or email me, whichever you prefer. Now get to class handsome." "Ok, I will." We exchanged text messages and spoke for a few days before she invited me back to her place. It was during the winter when I jumped on the bus and went to her home. She lived near the airport. When I arrived at the house, she was in the driveway and was having difficulty parking, so I helped her properly park her car. When I entered her fairly kept home, she was just as aggressive as the warden with snatching off my clothes and grabbing my stick-shift and parking it inside her space. She admitted, "Boy, you caught me at a great time. It's been three years and I was ready to explode." I just laughed and then gave her a massage. Round two and three were ok.

One day as Lloyd and I were walking the halls, I pointed her out to him while she worked in her office. "There she is, right in there." He hilariously said, "Huh no, that's where I draw the line bro. I'm not having sex with someone's grandmother. You're disgusting." I really don't recall how it felt being with Celeste, maybe because it was rushed. What I do recall is she sending me a text message, wishing me good luck on my exams, and saying that she would be taking a job offer in Virginia. During that summer, I took a Youth Violence course at the local community college. After using me as an example for inappropriate behavior between client and staff,

Professor Jane forcefully instructed, minutes before class ended, "Cornell, don't leave yet, I would like to chat with you," "Ok sure," while other students bombarded her with questions, she was short with them and repeated, "Cornell make sure you hang back after class." The other females just glanced at me and raised their eyebrows and when everyone left, Professor Jane and I simply walked to her car and chatted. I don't know what I was thinking, she clearly was interested and wanted me to fill in the blanks. I never delivered. We even exchanged a few text messages but nothing happened. My roster of women was just too full during that time but I certainly regret letting her get away. I saw her a few months later in the city, holding hands with another younger guy, and steam immediately began blowing out of my ears.

But here's a story that caused my jaw to hit the floor. In prison, I read an article about a female teacher being prosecuted for performing oral sex on a 17-year-old male student. Just prior to that date, the teacher had posted bail and was informed by the judge to stay away from all students for a previous allegation where she allegedly had sex with an 18-year-old from the same school. The 18-year-old mentioned that the teacher gave him oral sex in her car along with unprotected intercourse. The Judge spoke adamantly about the accusations, "I don't care if they're 17, 18, or 19. Just stay away. But the school allowed the teacher to return while the investigation was pending. The article went on to mention that the teacher mentioned to a female student that the 17-year-old was hot. The teacher then began receiving notes on her car entertaining her comments. The male student and the teacher began exchanging text messages which include sexual contact that was told to be erased by the teacher. The 18-year-old's claim was quite similar but was more in-depth about how the teacher would pick him up in her car and take him to his grandfather's house where the two would engage in sexual activity. She was given bail but finally suspended from the school. Now my first initial thoughts were, "Where the hell was this teacher when I was in high school?" The article mentioned that she was only 31-years-old, so I could only imagine her antics when she was a high school student. I think that the students are complete idiots and need to learn how to keep their damn mouths shut. I'm well aware of the moral dilemma, being unethical, and unprofessional but these are young men that willfully participated and pursued engaging in this matter. The fact that this educator allegedly violated company policy and smeared the image of the school easily warrants termination. But this is not a horrific forcible rape case and a conscious decision was made on the behalf of both parties. The fact that the students offered their consent should have led to a dismissal of this case. I feel sorry for the teacher who chose the wrong students to party with. I along with millions of other guys would have seen the bigger picture, while reaping all the benefits besides sex. A guaranteed excellent grade in her class along with a great letter of recommendation to a decent college would have been more to my benefit than a written statement to the police. You foolish clowns!

But I wasn't the only one making the prison my own personal brothel. It was no surprise when I heard that two female correctional officers were caught on camera having sex with two inmates and immediately escorted out of the building followed by their termination. Most famously when a female laundry worker from another prison, helped two convicted felons escape from a facility in upstate New York. After their month-long manhunt, I was rooting for the prisoners to get away with a media analyst stating that this jailbreak sounded like a movie. But one of the convicts was shot and killed by law enforcement and the other was safely captured. During the investigation, it was highly publicized that the female laundry worker was married but had an affair with one of the criminals she helped to escape. That wasn't a very good ending however, there was one situation that I truly respected. Another female officer was caught by her colleague giving oral sex to an inmate that was serving only a few years. Of course, the officer was fired but shortly returned to the facility and married the inmate while he was still incarcerated. I had to laugh because there was absolutely nothing the facility could do about it. After his release, the couple went on to have two children together. Now that's real jail love. But a psychologist had something different to say when writing an article about why female correctional officers chose to deal with inmates and why teachers choose to deal with students.

The Psychologist stated, "The majority of women are single mothers and have a void to be filled. The lack of attention and the day-to-day compliments if the inmate or student is that persistent certainly would become appealing because of the women's low self-esteem. This sort of correlation usually takes place between an inmate who has a job within the prison. Therefore, he has access to different departments of the facility that may require cleaning the guard's office a few times a week, bringing mail, or extra lunches for the hungry female who's been working a double shift and has not eaten all day. The inmate is in a well-placed position for him to cater to her needs. And for most women, it's the small things that really matter and of course that opens the door for flirting which is entertained by the C.O which leads to the inmate accomplishing the ultimate goal of sleeping with her. For some individuals, the thought of getting away with something that is prohibited fills that void. For female correctional officers, the feeling of control provides empowerment which is minimal, or nonexistent in their personal lives. It's not necessarily just for sex because sex can be obtained anywhere. It's a psychological issue. However, similar to correctional officers but slightly different for teachers who partake in these relationships, the student is not incarcerated and can easily transfer if he chooses to do so. Teachers have the same thought process of getting well-needed attention from the pupil and that they have full control of the situation. In all actuality, the student or inmate has control because he faces no detrimental consequences once the relationship is exposed. If not exposed, these matters usually end more badly for the teacher due to the student quickly losing interest and moving on to other territories as opposed to some much longer dealings between an officer and inmate because of him being incarcerated."

After reading, I then went into the rec room and saw Stewart, an older good-looking black guy with glasses in his early forties. Stewart always gave me the USA Today newspaper after he was finished. It was already well-known that he had an affair with a C.O for a full year but she quickly transferred before the jail had any proof. I asked about his experience. He was direct and even had a few choice words after reading the Psychologist's interview. "I don't give a damn who's in charge or that psychological garbage, what's most important is this chick bringing me anything that I needed or anything my homies needed. That being a cellphone so that I can call some of my other chicks. I smoke, so once in a while, I'd have her bring in some weed. I didn't want to make it a habit and have her bring in drugs and mess it up for myself and everybody else but those little tiny bottles of alcohol were appreciated. She took good care of a nigga. I told her to make sure to wear some strong ass perfume so I could smell her before she came on the unit. Hahaha. Sundays were the best because, during football, she would bring in huge platters of fried fish, mac and cheese, greens, spare ribs, and Kool-Aid for me and my friends. She wasn't that cute either but who cares. She was a dark-skinned, fat chick but her money was long. She used to tell me how her guy always cheated on her every time she surprised him with a new car because that wasn't the kind he wanted. Truth be told I would have cheated on her ass too. Hahaha. The jail was her escape from that crazy relationship because I made her feel appreciated. I use to counsel her than sex her down in the inventory room. But I played my cards right. One of my friend's names is Antonio. He makes really good cards; they look better than Hallmark cards. I would have him make her a card, then I would write something short and sweet. I dropped out of school in the eighth grade so I wouldn't be using any big words like this stupid Psychologist, sitting on the outside, trying to figure things out. I live this life. At one point I was dealing with two officers at the same time but the other one got fired for dealing with another guy. This jail life is like the street, they're not all whores but they exist. You just have to find the right one. But just a little word of advice Cornell, if you get into that situation don't tell anyone. Don't even tell your cellmate, don't even tell me."

CHAPTER 7

Like Father Like Son

DURING COLLEGE, I observed a much older gentleman taking an extreme liking to a younger guy, as the two were fellow students in my English class. I continued to observe them playing basketball together, although the older guy was in a wheelchair. I became more curious about their relationship after seeing them take lunch breaks together and working out in the gym room. Maybe I had fallen asleep or decided to cut class on the day that both gentlemen, being African American, announced that they were father and son. The value of education was instilled as both of David Sr.'s parents were teachers. In his earlier college days, he pursued a career path as an Engineer. Unfortunately, he dropped out of college to get a full-time job to support his newborn son, DJ (David Junior). David Sr. moved out and married DJ's mother Carmen. David Sr. worked a number of odd jobs and stayed clear of the law which they grew up in the tough streets of Pittsburgh but had recently relocated to attend the university. Over the years of doing back-breaking jobs and his knees having multiple torn cartilage, David Sr. had trouble walking and was placed in a wheelchair. He made it clear to the class that "Regardless of my handicap, I'm still blessed to be here with my son because I was going to give up. He's the one that encouraged me to keep fighting, so since I'm still here this is the best way to take full advantage of opportunities and accomplish my degree along with my son. I won't be able to work because of my ailment but I'm proud to have him as my successor."

DJ felt no burden and took pride in pushing his father around campus. He signed his father up for the handicap basketball program. His mother Carmen was in attendance at every game, cheering on her husband when they came in second place at the end of the season. David Sr. even went to a few college parties and took pictures with some of the drunk girls, sitting on his lap. He pushed his son to maintain a great standard of health and motivated DJ in the weight room. He never beat his son over the head with the word, but he always reminded DJ to "Always put God first in all that you do." His wife Carmen was there every step of the way and remained faithful to her husband. Both men spoke highly of their queen when admitting that every day wasn't pleasant but she was the crazy glue that held everyone together, whenever they bumped heads and didn't agree on certain issues. I really didn't see her often but she was nice looking and always helped to assist David Sr., inside the car when taking him to his doctor's appointments. However, when DJ decided to join the basketball team, you could see that the level of stress was taking its toll on her. Doctor's appointments, the gym, school, not to mention the cooking, cleaning, and personal care at home. Her hard work and commitment to her family would soon pay off. She was a trooper and did her duties willfully with a sincere heart. Both parents were always in attendance cheering on their son at every home game. Both men had done remarkably well at the university. I remember seeing David Sr., at the graduation and receiving his degree. Right after DJ received his degree, he was selected by the Boston Celtics in the second round of the NBA Draft.

In the penitentiary, rec time usually consists of guys playing chess, watching a movie, or sports on television. Others would spend several minutes talking to loved ones on the phone, or just relaxing and watching everyone do the previously mentioned. But one evening all activities were interrupted when a scuffle broke out between father and son. Both men were white and named Charles. They tried to rip each other's heads off but this wasn't the first time that they've gotten into a brawl. Other inmates were trying to enjoy the NBA finals so the fracas was quickly separated. But I guess words do hurt more than a fist. Charles Sr. offered a shocker, "I told your stupid ass momma to get a damn abortion, you hard-headed bastard. You want to act tough and gang bang? You're a bum, just like me." Charles Sr. was from Delaware; I heard from others that he ran out on his son's mother when she found out that she was pregnant. He worked odd jobs but would easily be fired for either not showing up, or just quitting until something else came along. He had no targeted profession and dropped out of high school in the ninth grade. He would beat his son's mother after she failed to give him money for alcohol and drugs. The majority of his life was spent in and out of prison for robbery and identity theft, all in which to support his habit. He even continued the same garbage in jail by stealing some of the inmate's pin numbers, so that he could use the phone in their name. He along with a few of his friends were known to steal another inmate's commissary after they would leave their cell to take a shower. Stewart, the guy that always gave me the newspaper, told me, "Man, that's really screwed up. Charles Sr., just turned 50-years-old, his son, CJ is 31-years-old and CJ's son is 12-years-old and he is in juvenile lockup for putting thumbtacks on a teacher's chair and for other crimes. Charles Sr. also has a brother, who's doing life for killing a guy during a robbery gone wrong." Amazed, I stated, "That's crazy, so basically all of the males in their family are incarcerated." "Yup, talk about carrying on the tradition."

CJ was part of the AB gang. Being spoken to in such a manner, I had a better understanding of his need of wanting to feel loved and accepted. "But hurting people was unacceptable." That's exactly what Ryan told him when he came to our fraternity. I was glad that he took the first step and came to us but CJ was a racist and he felt more comfortable speaking with Ryan. Similar to his father, CJ left his son's mother when the baby was 1-years-old. He'd been in and out of jail for numerous crimes but fortunately, he was there for a while and already had earned his G.E.D. So, after making the full commitment to join our fraternity, he and Ryan began studying some college-level material. He eventually got comfortable with me and told me that, "Man I used to do all kinds of crazy things. I raped a couple of chicks, I raped a few dudes on the street, I even raped a few dudes in jail." I just sat there and listened. I didn't say a word, I just listened as he continued to vent, "But my old man is lucky, he doesn't even know that although he didn't want me and told my mom to get an abortion," CJ tried his best to hold back tears but he started crying. He continued, "I saved his life, I saved his life Cornell because they were going to kill him. He stole from a couple of guys that had a life sentence, these guys don't have anything to lose and I just re-ordered all of the food that he stole from them." I assured CJ that, "Hey man, I know that had to be a tough move but you did the right thing." "No Nell, I should have let them do it. At least I have a good enough diploma, (GED). That fool doesn't even have one good sense."

There was an article written in the New York Times about a father and son, who had been sharing a jail cell for the last 15 years. They've been locked away from society in an upstate maximum-security prison in New York. The prison population houses 1,800 other inmates. The son was 42-years-old and Pop was 69-years-old. The son sleeps on the top bunk and pops, who suffers from a bad back, sleeps on the bottom. Behind a heavy steel door with a small set of bars, they would work on their appeals, write letters and watch football. Years prior to being incarcerated, they lived on a four-acre farm outside Syracuse, in rural Madison County. Now they occupy an 8x12 room. Officials with the state Department of Correctional Services said that this is a rare case. They said they did not know how many parent-child pairs were sharing cells in the prison system, which includes fifty-seven thousand offenders at sixty-seven facilities, because they do not track such data, but it is unusual for a father and a son to be in the same prison at the same time. In an interview, the son said, "It's crazy because while I was growing up, we used to fight all the time. It's a blessing because I get to keep my eye on him, now that he's a little older. I don't have to stress about his health issues or worry about people taking advantage of him." Overall, the deputy superintendent for security services found no fault with the arrangement. "I think it's odd that we have father and son as cellmates but my job is to keep a lid on the place. If I can find two people that get along well and double bunk, usually that means that I'm going to keep two more people out of trouble." The son's run-ins with the law started at 19 when he was arrested and jailed after he threatened neighbors with a 12-gauge shotgun and a knife because they refused to quiet down a loud party. The son then provoked a seven-hour stand-off with the county Sheriff's office that ended with the SWAT team throwing tear gas into the basement where he had been hiding.

At 18, He had dropped out of high school, lied about his age so he could begin working in restaurants. He then got married. Deputies had come to the house where he was staying with his wife to arrest him on misdemeanor assault charges after they had a fight. During this time, Pops was with his third wife and working in a bowling alley. Life for the son had begun to unravel as he moved back in with his father. In the summer of 1995, they were accused of embarking on a brief but violent string of robberies around the county that netted them only two thousand and nine hundred dollars in cash. They robbed a 61-year-old manager of the Salvation Army thrift shop in the town. Both father and son were charged with shooting the woman in her thigh and robbing her in a parking lot of the store as she carried a bag filled with seven hundred and twenty-six dollars to her car. The money was the day's proceeds from a sale of goods that had been donated to support the Salvation Army's drug and alcohol program. When investigators from three law enforcement agencies raided the duo's home after the robbery, they found a stockpile of rifles, pistols, knives, nunchucks, ammunition, and a police baton. It sounded like a plot from a movie as the two men pleaded not guilty to the charges. The jury deliberated about seven hours before finding them guilty of second-degree attempted murder, robbery, and other charges. On the day of the sentencing, the judge said that he suspected both men to be on the drug cocaine to support their habit because he couldn't find any other reason that they did this. Both men however showed remorse and stated that they made some really poor choices. The victim, the 61-year-old lady that was shot during the robbery, asked the judge to give them the maximum sentence. He did just that and handed down 25 to 50 years for both men. They were chained together and rode the bus to the prison together. After a few weeks, Pops wrote a letter to the superintendent, asking if he and his son could share a cell and it was granted.

I guess time would have to heal the pain between CJ and his father. I really just tried to focus on him being successful in the fraternity because this was his distraction from all of the stress. The hate level was really intense between the two. CJ would often avoid sitting at the same table with his father during mealtime and purposely never went to the yard whenever the old man mentioned that he would be going out to get some fresh air. Charles Sr. 's mother, who was 85-years-old, was able to make the eight-hour trip. She would have to visit them on two separate occasions because they even got into a fight during visiting hours and knocked the poor woman to the floor, which resulted in her needing a hip replacement. The lovefest continued, CJ's son was finally released from juvenile lockup and wanted to see his grandfather but out of spite, CJ wouldn't let him visit the old man. It gets better, after having enough of CJ's garbage, his father said to one of his friends, "Man it's not too late to have an abortion," and sure enough Charles Sr. tried to stab his own son during their next altercation. He just missed the jugular vein. Both men were again quickly restrained by other inmates because the jail had just gotten off lockdown for an inmate who stabbed a C.O then tried to commit suicide. Charles Sr., was an Atheist and often spoke out against Christianity, "If there is a God, then why doesn't he come to take this thorn out of my ass?" I almost replied, "If the good Lord that us Christians serve had done such a thing, you would not be alive." But I just glanced at him and smirked. He knew that I was very popular and was obviously trying to draw me into his conversation that was being held with his Klan friends. He continued, "God, God, God, it seems like the more people talk about this so-called God, it seems like there are more natural disasters." I just gave him a smirk, shook my head, and continued to read the newspaper.

When time permitted, I gave CJ a few words of encouragement. "You're actually in a great position to break this cycle CJ. You and I get out around the same time. But I need you to ask yourself this question tonight while relaxing in bed. "Who needs me more, my father or my 12-year-old son who just got out of jail?" He nodded as if he already knew the answer but the C.O blew the whistle and it was time for bed. Through personal experiences and lessons in the classroom, I had a better understanding of CJ's power struggle. Deep down he really loved his father regardless of the abandonment and the abuse but he also had to focus on himself so he could get back to his son. It's always sad when siblings are both incarcerated together but when father and son are suppressed, it's despicable. In this case, I guess prison saved both men from an early grave. Charles Sr., remained stubborn and refused to change. The next day I overheard him talking to his friends. "His mother drove me crazy, she'd nag me about my shoes being in the living room, plates in the sink, whatever the hell she could think of, so yeah I slapped her around a few times. She had to be taught a lesson on how to respect me as the man of the house. I actually got tired of beating her because she became immune to it and just sat and stared at me. Getting locked up was the best thing that could happen to me because she sent child support papers to my house. I didn't have to deal with her or her stupid, knucklehead kid." It took ten thousand angels in heaven for me not to chime in on CJ's behalf because I knew that he was hurting. It wasn't my place but I'm glad that during the conversation one of Charles's Sr. friends tried to talk some sense into him, but found it necessary to also trash the black man. "Man stop that garbage, stop acting like one of these stupid niggers. Niggers run out on their kids and have all them baby mamas. You don't have to deal with that nagging woman, especially now that he's a grown man, but that's still your boy." Charles Sr. was speechless as he and I then made fierce eye contact and I just chuckled and shook my head. He then walked over to me and said in his country accent, "You got something you want to say to me boy?" Before I replied, half of the rec room which was my fraternity brothers, stood up. We were a bunch of civil college guys but we certainly protected each other. I gently replied, "This clearly won't end well for you but your issue is with your son, not me sir, so just do what's right."

CHAPTER 8

Support

AFTER GRADUATING HIGH school by the skin of my teeth, everyone was extremely proud of me when I got my acceptance letter from college. Financial Aid didn't cover the entire cost for additional material and those chemistry books cost a pretty penny. Aunts, cousins, close friends were all there to provide assistants. It was sort of a big deal because being from a rough environment, not many young black kids attended college. I was blessed to not only attend a university but one of the best in the country. Both of my parents worked tremendously hard and it was my duty to deliver. During college, my mother sent me money, letters, and cards. Her warm words would instantly make me homesick. I remember when Kenny came to visit me and I snuck him into a few of the parties on campus. He mentioned how proud he was of me and admitted being a little envious because I had taken a different path to better my life. "Nell, I'm definitely jealous of you bro. Damn, I should have gone to college." On holidays when I returned home, the house was filled with family and friends. I was everyone's Christmas gift; I was the center of attention during thanksgiving meals as their overwhelming support became stifling. I didn't need a damn thing. My support system was the greatest. My reserve team, like Lloyd who came from a rich family, were busy either partying with his money or shoving it into my pocket just to make sure that I had a little something extra. But he took rejection as an insult. "No thanks Lloyd, I'm good bro." "Bro, take this or at least hold it for me just in case I spend too much tonight at the bar." "Ok gotcha."

One of the things that I most liked about Vanessa was her independence. She wasn't a pushover but never looked at me to pay a bill whenever we hung out. She was similar to Lloyd in that form which caused them both to bump heads. One night we all decided to go out to eat after class. When the bill arrived, the tussling began. "Your money's no good here Lloyd, I got it." He snatched the check while replying. "I already told Nell that this was my treat. So, I got it." She snatched it back while screaming, "Can you please just lower your ego for one freaking second?" I just sat in the middle of them both, then asked, "Well can I at least pay the tip? They both shouted "No" at the same time. She then tricked him. "Hey, Lloyd there goes your little boyfriend you slept with." When he turned his head, she snatched the bill out of his hand, then ran over to the bar and paid the bill while teasing him. "Ha Ha." Her aunt Ms. Carol played an essential role in my college success because she took a chance by allowing me to remain working, although my grade point average had fallen below the minimum. Ms. Carol was supposed to fire me but she gave me an opportunity and believed that I would get my act together. A true testament that a great key to being successful in life is to simply be nice to people and not burn your bridges, so I'm eternally grateful that I had a great relationship with her niece. During my sophomore year, I was on the verge of failing Intermediate Algebra for the second time. I simply came clean with my Turkish Professor, "Look, I'm not going to waste your time. I don't have the first clue what's going on in this class. I'm on academic probation and I simply need a satisfactory grade, so that I won't be dropped from the school." He replied, "Ok I understand, just do the best you can." I wrote my name on the paper and stupidly did some simple addition and subtraction. When the final grades were emailed, the Professor gave me a B grade in the course. Bless his heart. That was the highest grade on my transcript for the first two years. Unlike the other clowns who were plagiarizing every other assignment and trying their best to manipulate the system, I just came clean and was fortunate to be given a gift. But I wasn't the only one in school with a great support system. I saw other friends helping friends financially and kids jumping on the phone calling their parents asking for money, once they thought a five-hundred-dollar balance was a threat to their livelihood. One day I stood on the steps holding my books and waited for Lloyd to make a withdrawal and saw this white guy being pretty rough over the phone when asking his mother to send him some money so that he could party. "I only have five-hundred, measly dollars. Everyone else is hanging out with their friends, going to the clubs, and I'm stuck back at these stupid dorms. Can you please send me some more damn money before I lose my freaking mind, please?" His sense of desperation really just took me to an unimaginable, baffling place. Being a stubborn kid, I often bumped heads with my mother on many occasions. But I wouldn't dream of speaking to her in such a manner, especially having the nerve to request a favor in the same breath. I just shook my head and said "Wow."

During my trial and when the Judge read my verdict, the courtroom was basically empty. There were no friends, and no extended family members in the physical form to show support. I was never drenched with the feeling that anyone owed me anything but when you're down, that's when you know who's your real support system. There were no church members, letters, or visits from friends. My parents visited several times within the four-year sentence but my entourage faded. They didn't send me any money and words of encouragement. There were no photos sent of us hanging out in the bars and partying on campus. Those gestures could have brightened the few days that were dismal. The two dozen women that I was sleeping with were nonexistent. Making telephone calls was very expensive in prison, so I just corresponded with my family through letters. Through the grace of God, I never had to make an emergency phone call or receive one from the counselor's office. However, I felt bad for the grown men that I saw crying when calling home and asking their parents for money. "Well, can you just send me twenty bucks to get something extra to eat? I know that you got your social security check, or call aunt Georgia, it's Friday, I know somebody got paid." "Mom, dad just passed away, the damn insurance check had to be cleared by now." If they weren't embarrassed, I was embarrassed for them. Similar to college, you had your poor students and you had your poor inmates, who truly didn't have anyone to pick up the phone to make a request. Either their parents had died long ago or were just sick and tired of them being incarcerated every other year. But that wasn't my concern. My willingness to share the extra that was sent by my mother was much appreciated by myself and those who were less fortunate. It was my responsibility; it was how I was raised. If I had two of anything, I would give away one or break my bread in half to feed the hungry.

The staff support in prison was great. Mr. Phelps didn't have to leave the light on for me until my cell restriction was over. He could have easily said, "Too bad that's on you," and gave my seat to someone else that also needed to complete the course. Ms. Foley's contribution of providing me with the information for the state was critical. In return, there were days that I ran to the study room and I told her, "Hey just kick back and chill, I got this." "Are you sure Cornell?" "Yup, we'll run the show, go in the back and put your feet up, if we need anything, I'll let you know." "Thank you so much, Cornell, it's just one of those days, I really need to rest." Mr. Smith surely provided me with the extra favor of allowing me to select my own cellmate. The cafeteria workers were fond of my fraternity and my members consistently received extra portions during each meal. Having a great idea and dedication is good but nothing works without support. I was eternally grateful for Ryan, Justin, and Nate. And who could forget my new biggest fan in prison, the lovely warden who was now using me as if I was her own personal pogo stick three times a week, and swallowing my nutrients like a protein shake? I loved every moment. I was enjoying myself, but I wasn't greedy. I made sure that the warden gave each unit a pizza party twice a month along with movie night. The prison was happy. Stewart said, "Cornell when I first met you, I thought that you were a bit bougie.

You're the only guy in this entire facility wearing braces. You're always brushing your damn hair and looking in the mirror. These guys here think because they're in jail, they don't have to take care of themselves. Haha but you're cool. I can tell that you're as middle class as it gets." "Thanks Stewart, thank you for analyzing me." "No problem, Mr. Smooth. Here, my wife ordered me a year's subscription to GQ Magazines. They have some fly suits in there." "Wow, thanks, Stewart, yeah maybe a new style wouldn't hurt once I'm released." I still had two years remaining but the days were flying.

I had tons of support. This was the perfect place for folks to count their blessings instead of complaining about what's not going right in their lives. I was raised in the church from childhood. I made my own conscious decision to stray because of the way some of the heads in my church began operating and treating the people. But it was in prison that I reconnected with my spirituality. In my spare time, I would read the bible. I needed that spiritual support because this was a spiritual battle that I was facing. On paper my charges were, concealing a deadly weapon that committed a homicide but honestly, I knew God was holding me accountable for the other things that I managed to escape in the eyes of man. One Saturday night at School, Lloyd and another black guy, John, had brought home some Indian girls. These were some of the prettiest girls that I've ever seen in my entire life and they were completely intoxicated. Lloyd took one of the girls in one room and John undressed the other girl on the couch. I left to give them all some privacy but it wasn't long until I saw John leaving out and laughing. I went back to the room where it was pitch black and saw that the Indian girl was unconscious and sleeping in a puddle of vomit. Lloyd then looked in the room and started laughing. The next morning, I saw Lloyd walking down the hall with the two beauties. I then approached the one who had no knowledge of me seeing her defiled. "Hey beautiful, do you have a boyfriend? She looked at me and said, "Yeah, I have a white rich boyfriend, so I'm good." Lloyd and I just laughed at her stupidity as I simply just walked away. During another encounter with a beautiful blonde that Lloyd had slayed then jilted. As she slept, I quickly grabbed some condoms off Lloyd's dresser because I had a random acquaintance, who was supposed to be paying me a visit over at my place. Right before I tip-toed out of the room, the white girl finally awoke and looked me right in the eye and said, "Wow, I always wanted to sleep with a black guy but I know that this is a dream." She then flopped back down on the bed and I got the hell out of there.

Lloyd was rich but when we got drunk the foolery would have complete control. White folks in the local area kept the old fashion manner of leaving their doors unlocked at night. When leaving parties in the wee-hours of the morning Lloyd and I would playfully go into people's homes and steal money that was just left around. I was so surprised at how easy it was just to walk inside someone's home. In one house, I stood and watched a couple having sex and the woman brutally told the guy, "Ok, ok just stop. This is the worst." While glancing through the door, I almost burst out laughing. The woman quickly got up and began to get dressed, then walked past me in the hallway without noticing me or Lloyd, who was downstairs. We then ran out of the house. When we invaded another home, I saw a purse on the table completely filled with cash. I emptied it as Lloyd decided to expose our secrecy, and stood over an elderly, white couple and scared them half to death by screaming, "Clowns, clowns, clowns are everywhere." The horror on their faces was hilarious as they woke up and saw him standing over them. We ran down the street filled with amusement then bought more beer at a nearby 24-hour store. Soon as we approached the parking lot, I saw two police cars with the officers glancing at me. I then heard the call being dispatched about a home invasion that took place with two possible suspects on the loose. Both squad cars then took off in the direction of the home we had just left. We just looked at each other and burst out laughing but safely returned to his dorm and just chilled out for the rest of the day. Playfully sneaking into people's homes and stealing their money, cheating on Vanessa with multiple women, what the hell was I thinking? I was totally out of character and making poor, conscious decisions. This was indeed a spiritual battle and I deserved to be incarcerated. You reap what you sow. Incarceration was a much better therapeutic fit for me instead of a casket.

I missed Lloyd; he didn't deserve what happened to him but I was beginning to realize that certain pieces of the puzzle were forming based on how we were living our lives. Lloyd and I invaded people's homes and luckily, we were not shot and killed. But at the graduation party, Kenny went to Lloyd's home and shot and killed him. Incarceration was my karma. The prison was my support system to better my life moving forward. "One afternoon, while sitting in the yard, I told Ryan and Justin, "Like many others, we were not arrested, we were rescued." They looked confused as Justin asked, "Rescued?" "Yup, rescued from self-destruction. Luckily our crimes didn't make us famous and bring shame upon our prestigious universities. We were taken away from society quietly to reinvent ourselves." Ryan agreed "Yes, we were spared the relentless curse of Deuteronomy 28:15-68 for our disobedience." So, as I sat in my cell doing some soul-searching and evaluating my situation, that's when I picked up the Gideon's version of the Bible and began reading it for a half-hour a day. The chapel was always packed with a diverse group. The welcoming and thoroughly sung, "Break Every Chain" by the men's choir rejuvenated my soul. It's a really touching song. As I glanced around the chapel and saw others crying on their knees and repenting for their sins. Pastor Phillips, a bald-headed, tall black man who was an ex-con and drug addict, always followed up with a heartfelt but candid message of "We have to learn to take responsibility for our own actions. We're in control. The moment we decide to stray from the Lord's will and lose control, then we offer someone else to be in control of us."

CHAPTER 9

Difference

IT WAS IN college that I had my first experience with an atheist. Everyone is entitled to their own beliefs and I'm certainly not the best Christian but it was just surprising to me, to hear so many people being cynical. Completing an elective course was a requirement, so I chose Philosophy 101. As Vanessa and I walked from the cafeteria on a beautiful sunny day, she warned me, "I took that class, if you're sensitive about your religion, then it's definitely not for you. So, brace yourself." Professor Bolt briefly explained his journey and finally his conversion to atheism. "I grew up as a catholic, then tried the protestant thing for a while then back to Catholic and when all the scandals broke out with the priest using the little boys as their sex toys and the church trying to cover it up, that was pretty much it for me." I would often overhear the atheists in their circled group meetings on campus. One white girl stated, "When I finally decided to convert to atheism, it was such a relief that I didn't have anyone watching over me and judging me." Another white guy corrected her, "No see, that's the scam about Christianity and all of these other so-called religions that teach about a false savior protecting you from harm. Where is this savior when a gunman decides to walk into a room filled with kids and start shooting?" Another guy asked? "Yeah, is this so-called God blind or deaf? These incidents are happening over and over again, giving him more opportunities to finally show up." The circle continued as another gentleman stated, "And the stupid idiots give thanks to him whenever something good happens in their lives." During this time, I had known that atheists didn't believe in God but I didn't know that they also don't believe in the devil. I also didn't know that there were two different kinds of atheists. Not that I cared to know for personal reasons but since I did in fact sign up for the class, I did a little research. As far back as 1772, Baron D, Holbach said that "All children are born atheist; they have no idea of God." Atheism is about belief, or specifically what you don't believe. Agnosticism is about knowledge, or specifically about what you don't know. An Agnostic doesn't know if any Gods exist or not.

Whenever a student would make a case for their own religion, Professor Bolt's go-to questions were, "How do you know? Were you there?" Did you actually see Jesus raise Lazarus from the dead and give sight to the blind? Or how about the time he supposedly walked on water? I shocked him and the entire class by mentioning, "Well that's certainly more believable than the earth starting from nothing and that we were formed from atoms. Even the well-known atheist, Antony Flew ultimately renounced atheism. He changed his mind in 2004 when announcing he had come to believe in God. He even wrote a book called "How the World's Most Notorious Atheist Changed His Mind. It's a pretty good book, Professor, you should check it out." He was speechless and merely replied, "Ha, I see." I was impressed with Flew's innovative views. According to www.strangenotions.com, Antony Flew elaborated that, "There were two factors in particular that were decisive. One was my growing empathy with the insight of Einstein and the other noted scientists that there had to be an intelligence behind the integrated complexity of the physical universe. The second was my own insight that the integrated complexity of life itself which is far more complex than the physical universe-can only be explained in terms of an intelligent source. I believe that the origin of life and reproduction simply cannot be explained from a biological standpoint despite numerous efforts to do so. With every passing year, the more that was discovered about the richness and inherent intelligence of life, the less it seemed likely that a chemical soup could magically generate the genetic code. The difference between life and non-life, it became apparent to me, was ontological and not chemical. The best confirmation of this radical gulf is Richard Dawkins' comical effort to argue in *"The God Delusion"* that the origin of life can be attributed to a lucky chance. No, I did not hear a voice. It was the evidence itself that led me to this conclusion."

Professor Bolt was impressed after mentioning a week later before class started, "Huh, young Richards, it seems as though we're never too old to be educated. That was an interesting read that you recommended but unlike Flew, I will be remaining an atheist and standing my ground of my disbelief in your God. Now class, please turn your textbooks to chapter three." I just smirked and opened my book as the professor continued. "How many of you were born into your religion?" Half of the class raised their hands. How many of you converted to another religion after reaching a certain age when having a better understanding of your faith? A quarter of the class raised their hands. "Now to be honest, how many of you felt like you made a mistake, leaving your original faith and wanting to reconvert? Almost half of the class raised their hands. He was surprised, "WOW." One white, young lady admitted, "I just feel as though not believing in anything is similar to not having a purpose in life. For instance, if I don't believe in God then how am I supposed to believe that someone is going to tell me the truth or a bad situation is going to get better? Atheism is basically telling us to rely on a man. Well, what makes one man better than the next?" I saw the Professor's answer coming, I said every word as he was speaking. "Don't you rely on a man to keep your neighborhood safe from rapists, burglars, robbers?" "You rely on a man to make those fancy little shoes you're wearing and that pretty little dress. My next question is optional but don't you traditionally rely on a man to insert his penis inside of you, and to have healthy sperm so that you can have a beautiful family? That's the power of Atheism, we rely on our human nature and intelligence, not on a God that shows up when it's convenient. The young lady was speechless. Professor Bolt was loose with the tongue and he often bumped heads with some of the Muslim students.

One African American, male student proclaimed, "But Muhammed teaches us about brotherhood, and our great leader, Louis Farrakhan has been exceptional." I couldn't wait for this reply; I knew that the heat was coming. The Professor chuckled, then issued, "Muhammad ok. But are you kidding me? The same Mr. Exceptional stated just recently in an interview that he believes in segregated relationships and that whites are going down if they don't stop mixing with the blacks. He also predicted that there will be no more white people by 2050 if they don't stop integrating with the blacks. At least, President Obama had enough sense to denounce his endorsement back in 2008." The Muslim student then slammed the book on the desk and stormed out of the room while grumbling, "I'm dropping this stupid class." The Professor hilariously informed him, "Well you better hurry up because tomorrow is the deadline." After the student exited the room, Bolt asked, "Be honest, how many of you feel unsafe and fear that he might return and shoot up the class?" Half of the class raised their hands. "Although he didn't make any threats it's better to be safe than sorry, so I'll still report him to security." I then asked, "Professor, what is the correct term or is it possible for someone to practice two different religions at the same time?" He was surprised again, and replied, "Great question Cornell, the answer is Syncretism. Also, as it relates to your question the term Omnism, or Omnists means belief in all religions. These are the people that say all religions contain truths, but that no one religion offers all that is true." I was intrigued and did additional research and found that a story was published about a female Reverend from Seattle, who the director of faith formation and a priest for 20-years had surprisingly told her congregation that she was also practicing Islam after an introduction to Islamic prayers left her profoundly moved.

The article continued to startling mention that on Friday afternoons, the Rev., ties on a black headscarf, preparing to pray with her Muslim group, then on Sunday mornings, she puts on the white collar of an Episcopal priest. I couldn't help but laugh at what most people would call a great state of confusion. Even as I typed these words, I found these acts to be quite tickling. She confirmed that these rituals are consistently done because she is both "Muslim and Christian and that they are the same." That statement certainly is not true because Christians believe that Jesus is the son of God and Muslims regard Jesus only as a prophet. Furthermore, the Bible says that our God is a jealous God and we should not worship any other Gods. After reading the article, I highly anticipated the hilarious comments.

"So, I guess she thinks the Stanley Cup and The Riders Cup are the same." LOL.

"It's like being a Republican and a Democrat at the same damn time."

"Double Jeopardy, nice spot in hell awaits you."

"Shame on the church for not removing Krusty the Clown." LOL.

"I will be praying for this person that she knows God through Jesus. Those of us who know God through Jesus let's not stone her but pray for her salvation."

Reading this garbage left me questioning myself about who was more confused, the Atheist or the folks practicing Syncretism? I recall having a brief encounter with an Atheist, she was white with long gold hair. We met on the subway, during my spring break as I waited for the train on my way home. When we went out for dinner, I completely turned her off because I prayed before eating my food. She laughed then asked, "If there is a God, why would you have to ask him to bless your food? Why couldn't he just prevent anything from happening to it in the first place or does he just like to get his ass kissed?" I almost flipped over the table but I just took a deep breath and answered, "It's a wonderful part of our tradition to pray and give thanks for what has been provided for us." She rolled her eyes but after dinner, she asked me to go home with her. It was the first time in my adult life that I turned down sex. Come to think of it, I saved myself some embarrassment because I knew that the chances of me being aroused were slim. However, the Atheist taught me a valuable lesson about psychological compatibility and that sex was not just a physical aspect. People who think alike, usually are friends and get along well with each other. I had to brace myself for the philosophy course as Vanessa suggested and received a satisfactory grade in the fifteen-week course, but my two-hour dinner date with the Atheist was strangely more personal and impactful because of the immediate assessment, and possibilities of being the significant other of such a person.

One day as I relaxed by myself in my cell, it dawned on me that there were more intelligent, non-believers than intelligent believers of Christ. The fact of the matter is there are some really stupid, ignorant people in prison. The same could be said for the free society but of course, a point will be made. There were dozens of inmates that had been in jail for almost 20 years and could not read. They would go to church every Sunday, listen to their favorite songs on the radio, gossip and believe the freshly planted lies and even have a job in the kitchen. How can someone be that active, and not know how to pick up a book with general information, and learn how to read it from front to back? I recall when being in Mr. Phelps's class he said, "I don't know what the hell is wrong with some of you guys. That library is filled with over five thousand books and they won't even read them. Years ago, folks would be strung up by trees if caught trying to read, now the books are being offered to you and you won't read them." I had to agree. These were the same guys who were giving God thanks for allowing them to see another day but they failed to educate themselves with the FREE tools that the good Lord provided for them. It was perplexing but more so how the white Atheist was always reading, keeping calm amongst themselves or their small group. They shared their food, and cigarettes even with religious believers. I saw them intensely studying the Bible just so they could continue to throw shade and rebuke the word of God or perhaps, surprisingly convert to Christianity. The majority of them had graduated high school and attended college but dropped out. We never debated our religious differences but Ryan was fortunate to convert a few skinheads to our fraternity, and I also welcomed them with open arms.

I found peace when returning to the church services. Instead of viewing it as a place that scolded you with the word, Sunday morning was my chill time. I felt cleansed. Prior to this time, I hadn't been to church in two years. It felt good again just to relax and listen to the melodies of "Glory Glory, Hallelujah" from the men's choir. I was now at the halfway point of completing the Bible. It was like a history lesson. The stories that were told to me as a child were a bit graphic but more comprehensive. This comprehension ushered me to ponder getting baptized again because I was forced to do so at age 16 by my parents. Especially from my mother. "Cornell, when are you getting baptized? Cornell the baptism is in two months, I'll let the Pastor know to put your name on the list, Cornell please give your heart to the Lord. Cornell, when are you getting baptized? I finally did it in 1999, so she could leave me the hell alone. Did I backslide since my teenage years, absolutely but a second initiation wasn't necessary? I would repent by asking God for forgiveness through prayer and changing my promiscuous manner, my consumption of alcohol and usage of marijuana, and removing profanity from my extensive vocabulary. I was inspired to further do so when witnessing others make the transformation. Phillips was the Pastor, but I had to practice what I preached. If I wanted gang members to convert to college life, I had to lead by example and reintroduce myself back to Christianity. I wasn't suffering from an addiction but having zero participation was just as difficult because I had supernatural access when my good friend, the warden, mentioned, "Anything you need baby, weed, Hennessey, vodka, whatever your choice of drink is I gotcha." My life was completely perfect on the inside. I never smoked marijuana in prison but after sex, the warden would make us a few drinks on ice. But I got back to reading my Bible. I laughed for days when reading the curse of "A person being fed ten loaves of bread and still wouldn't be full." LOL!

CHAPTER 10

What's on the Menu?

ACCORDING TO THE Journal of American College Health, "A survey was taken in 2019 of 1,738 college students aged 18 to 27 years old. The study showed 95% of the teenagers were overweight and obese. For the 20-year-old's, a rate of 21% was overweight. More valuable information was found on mustangnews.net where a study found most college campus foods to be unhealthy. The study was released in 2019 after being sent to the Center for Disease Control and concluded that only 12% of the three-hundred and sixteen entrees are in good health. The research team used the Nutrition Environment Measures Survey for Campus Dining to analyze all dining locations. This system of measuring healthy food is used around the entire country. The highest range of scoring is 97 and 4 is the lowest. When these numbers were revealed, students expressed their concerns.

"Having 12% of entrees considered as healthy just makes me wonder what the hell have I been eating?"

"So college has been feeding me 85% of garbage? No wonder I felt sluggish during classes."

"That's exactly why I buy all the food I eat from the grocery stores. I can't stand on-campus food because it isn't healthy and nutritious. The selection is limited and very expensive. I've been buying food from Trader Joe's and cooking all of my meals. I make it for the complete goal of not eating on-campus food."

"Now some colleges have the nerve to partner with fast food companies to have their restaurants on campus to continue fattening us up, while their accounts get fat. These universities don't give a damn about us."

After the study was issued, the administrator from a college who was in charge of campus dining stressed how difficult it is to feed a university and the improvements that have been made. "We make nearly twenty thousand meals a day, we've hired a registered dietician to help influence menu development. The long-term goal for campus dining is to have a "Made-in-front-of-you" method of preparing the food for the students. A VG café, where students can choose ingredients and customize their orders would be more beneficial for those who are more conscious about what they eat." I then did additional research to see if I could find any books written for college students that wanted to better their diet and found some really great options. "The Dorm Room Diet," by Daphne Oz, "Mindful Eating 101: A Guide to Healthy Eating in College and Beyond," by Susan Albers, and "College Cooking," by Megan and Jill Carle. On a beautiful day in the Spring. Myself, Vanessa, and Lloyd relaxed, smoking in a park right off-campus. Vanessa asked, "So guys, we're juniors now with only one more year. What are you two going to miss the most about college?" We both looked at each other and said "Wawa" then laughed. We ate like pigs in college. I rarely had a proper breakfast meal. Once in a while, I would grab a cereal bar but for the most part, I was always on the run. I wasn't that big on beef but it was still terrible when a chicken cheesesteak was the first meal of the day. We lived at Wawa, purchasing junk food to satisfy our intense cravings after smoking weed and getting drunk on Friday nights. My lunch always consisted of the honey buffalo wings, pizza, cheese fries, pasta, and Chinese food. I loved to eat turkey sandwiches with lettuce and tomatoes but the bread had a lot of carbs. As a matter of fact, I only ate chicken and broccoli with carrots, when ordering out on the weekends. For the most part, a bottle of wine or some sort of fruity alcoholic beverage that contained tons of calories was featured during my lunch and dinner meals. During my four years in college, I must have gotten high hmm… let's say on average three times a week. There are 52 weeks in a year so 3x52= 156. That's 156 times in 1 year. Four years of college, so 156x4= 624. So, I got high 624 times during my four years in college. I know for sure that after every time we smoked, we binged. That means I binged, ate 624 times and only weighed 161 pounds, and was completely healthy. God has been good to me. This isn't counting the times that I smoked marijuana during my teenage years, which I started at age 13, with my neighborhood friends. The intense cravings were massive side effects but so were the enjoyable laughs.

I love to eat. You really have to screw up food for me not to enjoy it. My favorite starches are rice and potatoes. I find it most delightful when a beef stew is poured over the rice with a tall glass of iced tea and dinner rolls. I love when spaghetti is properly cooked with ground turkey, garlic bread along with broccoli. I'm always up for some baked chicken, carrots, or string beans. I'll never turn down a well ripe orange, cantaloupe, or watermelon when having my breakfast, lunch, or dinner. Peaches and pears are my favorite desserts. As I write these pleasurable, mouthwatering meals, I'm contemplating taking a break, so that I can call up a lady friend and place my order. I don't know what the hell the other inmates in Coal Township were complaining about but the food was not too bad. They served the generic version of my previously mentioned favorites. But I guess being served the same thing every day for the past twenty years is a reason to complain. I was considered a short-timer because my sentence was under five years. Along with the mandatory three meals a day, I still ate some of the jailhouse meals prepared in the rec room. Ramen Noodles mixed with whatever meat that was served from an earlier dinner. The seasoning packs were very salty and filled with sodium, so I was careful when applying them to my food. But at times the lunch or dinner that was served in the chow hall was so bland, I would take a seasoning pack with me to wake up the insipid meal.

Other inmates would boil the noodles in a clear trash bag, then add crunched-up Doritos, Sour Cream and Onion Chips, BBQ chips, Cheese Puffs, Nacho Cheese, sausage meat and eat it with bread. It's called a "Chi-Chi." It looks absolutely disgusting, similar to three days' worth of vomit. However, after watching a Puerto Rican inmate from a distance ardently prepare the slop, he invited me to dine. His name was Hoover, he had just converted to our fraternity from the MS 13 gang and also recently had gotten Baptized. He wanted to cook for us to celebrate the beginning of his new righteous journey. It was a celebration and I didn't want to be rude, so I joined in along with Ryan and Justin. I was impressed, the Chi Chi was actually pretty good. Hoover explained, "It's all about moderation Papi, and how you choose to do it. You don't have to use all that extra stuff. You can even make a healthy Chi-Chi with vegetables like corn, beans, broccoli. Whatever you want to do. Just add a little seasoning pack for flavor." It was similar to the famous bowl that KFC used to serve with fried popcorn chicken, corn, mash potatoes, and gravy. Maybe the chicken bowl from Chipotle tops them all because of the touch of guacamole. Oh, how I loved it so much and it really made me realize how much of the little toppings solidified the entire meal. For the most part, the meals were average in prison. The commissary list was loaded with junk food which I would certainly indulge with ordering at least two boxes of my chocolate "Nutty Bars." I would mainly order just the Ramen Noodles because they were filling and the chicken flavor was the best. The extra packs of Kool-Aid and iced tea were excellent thirst quenchers along with a few bags of trail mix to satisfy my late-night munchies. But just as Hoover instructed us to do, "Everything in moderation." I also worked out every day and drank a lot of water.

What a coincidence, my favorite childhood rapper "Prodigy" of Mobb Deep, released a cookbook. Prodigy was rich and after a legendary career that started from his early teens, his Platinum and Gold albums certifies the well-deserved recognition. He was arrested in 2007 for illegal gun possession and sentenced to 3 1/2 years in jail and was released in 2011. He came a long way from the gritty streets of Queens Bridge, New York. Now with attempts to create another classic, his cookbook, *Commissary Kitchen* educated fans on his experience about the food and cooking his own meals while being incarcerated. The book was released in 2016. Prodigy explained during the introduction, "In a world where prisoners are treated like animals, we made our experiences there feel more human by how we prepared our food." Eating healthy was important to Prodigy due to his sickle-cell anemia. He admits to not being much of a chef but wanted to take more control of his situation. In the chapter, "Prison Surprise," Prodigy also had an interesting, but more health-threatening experience when eating the Ramen Noodles. He agrees with me that "It looks disgusting," but afterward suffered a severe case of food poisoning that landed him in the infirmary with an IV in his arm. I was fortunate not to experience any of the horrors that my childhood idol had endured. However, Prodigy gave fans his top three worst prison food experiences which the previously mentioned was the first one. The second incident occurred when he was getting ready to eat dessert. "The bread pudding that was being served had a pubic hair sitting out, in the middle of it like a birthday candle." I was on the floor and almost died with laughter. Such humor! I've heard stories such as the workers pouring urine in the apple juice and spitting in the grits but I honestly still ate my food but said my grace before doing so. In the book, Prodigy also agrees with me that the commissary list is full of garbage but inmates still order from it to prevent hunger.

The third incident he experienced was hearsay but came from a reliable source. There was a cooler filled with juice. After everyone had drunk all of the juice, they found a dirty dishrag at the bottom of the cooler. Not as funny as his second mishaps but if there was any truth to that story, that's just downright terrible and I hope no one got sick, except for the clowns that made the juice. Karma always makes its way around. Prodigy also expressed his frustration after hearing the face cringing tale. "There's a bunch of crazy, sick people in jail. You hear stories like that all the time, where inmates do weird things to the food." He provides a breather by mentioning for inmates who are more conscious about their diet can have food delivered from family but it can't weigh over fifty pounds. Prodigy's music was heavenly influential during my teenage years and now as an adult, his cookbook was just as influential and inspiring to begin having a healthier diet. I don't have sickle cell anemia or any other generic blood disease and I surely don't need to have one to see that this masterpiece expresses growth and maturity while educating those behind bars about making better choices when it comes to YOUR LIFE. He stated, "Making your own food in prison brings people together and surely makes the time go faster. You almost forget where you are until you wake up the next morning for the count." He credits daily exercising in the jailhouse gym and yard workouts which were great supplements to a healthier lifestyle. I'm confident that he had access to a gym before his incarceration, but like myself, we pressed the issue due to our circumstances. "Survival of the fittest, only the strong survive." Mobb Deep, Shook Ones Album.1995

A complaint was brought to my attention from Hoover in regards to needing extra time to work out. I still kept our relations under wraps and the next time that I saw my girl, that favor was also granted. This was a time to not only help others but to utilize my time and enhance my physical temple. I would lift weights outside with a little motivation from the big boys. "Come on, one more Nell, Come on, one more." These guys looked like bodybuilders. I mainly did calisthenics and was impressed with how my body immediately responded and began to morph within three weeks. But I need to get back to my routine. I got so content and accustomed to the attention that I haven't worked out in a year because I still have the results from my incarceration. In college, I never worked out. If I was in the gym, it was only to hang out and gawk at the sexy girls getting toned on the treadmill. That was Vanessa's favorite machine. Every morning and sometimes in the evening, she would sit in the corner after having a health shake then pound away at the treadmill. She tried to encourage me. "Come on slacker, join me." I should have known better, but I tried to look impressive. "This is a piece of cake." I didn't even know which buttons to push but she adjusted it for me to start at a respectable pace. After a couple of minutes, I almost passed out and hilariously stumbled off the treadmill. The other girls laughed at me as Vanessa helped me gather my belongings then I made a quick exit. It was shortly after that I decided to keep my distance from the gym room. But I got a pretty good useful tip from wikihow.com. "Run or walk on the treadmill until you reach at least seventy percent of your maximum heart rate. The American College of Sports Medicine, says that when you hit this target, you maximize the amount of fat and calories you burn." I didn't remember the numbers that Vanessa hit but Hoover joined me in the gym and he advised, "Papi, just start off at a slow pace. Get your legs used to it and build up your wind strength, then you'll be fine. The gym room was small and musky, and I really didn't feel comfortable being in there by myself whenever Hoover wasn't there. There was too much tension from those other big muscle guys from other units that were constantly staring me down. Not cool! So, I just ran a few laps around the track and did my pushups out in the open where everyone could be properly supervised.

CHAPTER 11

Life

IT WAS NOW the summer, and after performing poorly in the spring semester of my junior year, I decided to take a couple of summer classes at the local community college to keep the ball rolling. Failure was not an option. I re-registered for a Political Science class which my first attempt resulted with an F grade. I saw a familiar face in the class but I was uncertain. When the fat, white obnoxious Professor, named Mr. Burt, asked everyone to quickly introduced themselves, my memory was confirmed when Mr. Abdul Safar, an African American, mid-age Muslim, gentlemen, stated that he previously worked in a telemarketing agency for several years. I worked at that same agency when I was 18-years-old. We were supposed to be selling life insurance and credit protection but we would sweeten our pitch when contacting potential customers and telling them that they simply had to review the policy and that it came along with a free television or a car. They believed us, we laughed and collected bonuses and they got a bill in the mail for hundreds of dollars for not canceling the free subscription after 30 days. Oops, I guess we forgot to mention that part. It's been a few years since I saw Mr. Safar, so I reintroduced myself to him after class. "Mr. Safar, hey it's Cornell from the telemarketing agency." "Heyyy Cornell, young brother, you're looking well?" "Thanks, so how've you been?" I asked. "Just taking it one day at a time Cornell. The thing that I've learned about myself is that I work much faster at a much slower pace." "That's interesting, how so?" "Well take a look around Cornell, everyone is always in a rush, whether it's their job, kids, school, friends. Everyone is always in a rush. The mistake I made was trying to keep up the pace with everyone else." "You mean, life in general?" "Yeah." We ordered some lunch from a food truck then sat down on the benches outside of the school. I then asked, "So how is school working out for you so far?" "It's actually my first semester and I decided to major in Communications." "That's great Mr. Safar." "Yup, I'm going all the way to the top. I'll get my Doctorates, I'm 45-years old now and I've decided to be a lifetime student and take one class a semester."

"Wow, that's going to be a pretty interesting journey sir." "Yup, but enough about me, how are you, Cornell?" "I'm over at the university, it's a challenge, I'm just here for the summer to rack up on some more credits." He then teased, "You should do well con-man, hahaha." "Oh, I'm the con-man? You taught me everything I know, hahaha." We then admitted it was fun while it lasted as the telemarketing agency went bankrupt and finally closed down. When we parted ways, I first thought that Mr. Safar was a complete idiot and basically the definition of an old fool. He mentioned being 45-years-old and wanted to acquire success at the highest level. So, it would make more sense to accomplish such a feat with the time he had, being at such an advanced age. One class a semester, do you know how long that's going to take? That's what I wanted to ask but his philosophy of being a lifetime student satisfied my curiosity. Since I was more curious about the numbers, I went online and did a little research and saw that it would probably take Mr. Safar almost 20 years to get his Bachelor's degree, another 10 years for his Master with an additional 10 years for his Doctorates. If Mr. Safar was to stay on track and not slack off on his goal for one class per semester. He would be 85-years-old when accomplishing his Doctorates degree. Due to his well-seasoned age, his employment opportunities would be shot, but he could open his own practice and provide others with an opportunity to carry on his name. After inquiring online about Mr. Safar's philosophy, one student graduated from Iowa State University after taking one class a semester. She first enrolled in 1992. Forty semesters later, the 48-year-old woman finally graduated 19 years later with an Accounting Degree. Other students online found that a slower pace was more beneficial, not as slow as Mr. Safar but opposed to the rat race of graduating on time.

"My grades are much better when deciding to take a lighter load of only three classes per semester plus I work 5 days a week."

"Most employers don't care how long it took you to graduate."

"A lot of people put pressure on themselves to graduate in four years like it's high school. college is totally different because of life taking its course. Some people need to make money and postpone or attend school part-time so a slower pace is justifiable."

"So, what if it takes you 7 seven years, in 7 years you will be older. You can be 7 years older without a degree or 7 years older with a college degree. It's a no-brainer, get the degree, no matter how long it takes."

This was some pretty good motivation. If it wasn't for the community college as a safety net, it might have taken me 20 years to get my degree. I failed a lot of classes but I also passed a lot of classes then always took summer courses to make up for the ones I failed. My best years academically were during my junior year when I received a satisfactory grade in all three of my fall semester courses. I was on a roll. I had my own philosophy. I didn't give a damn if your G.P.A was a 10.0 and you had all the scholarships in the world. At the end of the day, as long as we're walking next to each other down the aisle at the graduation ceremony, that's all that matters. The question on the job application is going to ask, "Did you graduate?" and we're both going to be able to check "Yes" in the column section. However, I'm vigorously pursuing my author career, so the only box I'll be checking is the mail for my royalty checks.

I was now at the halfway point in my prison sentence and while I sat reflecting on the previous two years, my cellmate, Dexter asked, "Cornell, since this is your very first time in a state penitentiary, what were you most afraid of?" "Hmm.. Well, if I was afraid of anything, it was more shocking when I first met Willie Beckman. "Old head Willie who works down in inventory when you first arrived off the bus?" "Yup", "But he's cool," Dexter said. "Yeah, he's cool now that they have him locked up. Willie was the first person that I've ever met that had a life sentence. He was a pretty vicious dude." "Please, do tell." "When I first arrived at Coal Township with another twenty guys, we sat in the inventory room for a couple of hours. During that time, there was a young, loud-mouth Puerto Rican kid, class clown, who kept cracking jokes and thinking the facility was going to be a piece of cake. "Man, this is going to be sweet. I'm only here for ten years, it's going to fly." I blocked out the clown by putting my head in my lap but moments later, a baritone voice entered the room and interrupted the joker but also got my attention. "You better shut the hell up and stop making all that damn noise in here. You stupid, little knuckle-head." The voice demanded everyone's attention. "You think this is a damn playground, it's idiots like you that come in here with a ten-year sentence but don't live past two years."

Willie Beckman, was a notorious truck driving, drug dealing, murdering, rapist from the eighties. He did this over the span of a 15-year-career. It was easy for him to get away, being that truck drivers rarely got pulled over. He would brutally rape or kill his victims, stash them inside of the truck, then drop them off in another state before reaching his final destination. He was supposed to be delivering steel and wood for contractors to build houses but Willie made it his business to stop in the local bars and party. Being a mixture of Hispanic and African American, Willie was quite appealing to women. After entertaining his frail victim with clever conversation and alcohol, a few women ended up being dismembered and stuffed in the woods. His truck driving career paid fairly well but tons of extra cash after making coke deals with some local pushers were always welcomed. His $80,000 yearly salary later became chump change. Willie was making an additional three-thousand a week with drug deals, bringing his total to almost two hundred thousand a year. Not a bad payday for the murdering bachelor. He once traveled across the state to collect some money from some Italians, the guy thought that Willie was a pushover and tried to show off in front of his two other friends by shorting Willie ten bucks and insulted him. "It's only ten bucks, you bum, beat it." Willie then replied, "Ok man, not a problem." Willie then walked back to his truck, and seconds later returned with a blow torch and threatened to throw gasoline on the guy, if he didn't pay up. "Give me my damn money. Now." Completely terrified, the guy nervously pulled twenty dollars out of his pocket and gave it to Willie, but Willie still threw the gasoline and lit him up with the blow torch, just to teach the other guys a lesson. They fled but not before also throwing money at Willie. But he just left it on the ground, so it could look like a robbery gone bad. He sparked up a cigarette and strolled back to his truck and took off down the highway.

His demise finally surfaced after viciously beating and raping one of his victims. He passed out after thinking she was dead. The woman managed to escape the attack and after going to the authorities, she later found out that she was pregnant. She testified how Willie almost killed her but glad a life was created and that she didn't believe in abortions. She gave birth to a beautiful baby girl but gave her up for adoption because she did not want to raise that monster's child. Talk about forgiveness and reconciliation. His daughter Rochelle, grew up to be a very beautiful and successful young lady, who works with Veteran's Affairs. She looked him up in the system then reached out to him after a DNA test proved that he was indeed her father. She's the only family member he has and she's been a tremendous support system. She's so remarkable that she even wrote letters to his judge requesting for him to be released and reported the progress that he's made over the years. That late afternoon after Willie harshly scolded the playful Puerto Rican, Willie confirmed, "And for those of you who want to know, I've been here for 42 years." The judge scheduled a hearing because there was an error made on the court's behalf during his sentencing. Willie was summoned by the court because his sentence was supposed to be for 106 years and 30 days. The judge only gave him 106 years, so he was summoned to court along with his daughter and the error was corrected with the Judge denying all her appeals that were filed and gave Willie the additional 30 days on top of his 106-year sentence. Damn! He went from making almost $200,000 dollars a year to 12 cents an hour, handing out clothes and other personal items to inmates. He was able to get a pretty good lawyer after the prosecutor rounded up all of the evidence from blood trails, DNA, fingerprints, the saws that were used to cut up the victim's bodies, and the multiple guns that were found in his cheap motel. He was found guilty but eluded the gas chamber due to expressing remorse for his crimes." As I retold the story of Willie Beckman, I could see the horror on Dexter's face as he then took a deep breath and drank a cup of water.

He was a very dangerous man but I took it upon myself to get to know Willie Beckman. I knew that he worked the morning shift so after lunch, I walked over to the inventory department, where he was instructing a new correctional officer where to properly place the inmate's name charts. I pretended to be thirsty and got a drink of water, then introduced myself. "Hello Mr. Beckman, I'm Cornell, I live in the C unit. "Hey kid, nice to meet you. I know it's a sign of respect but you can just call me Willie." "Ok cool." "So, Cornell, where are you from out there in the world?" "I'm from West Philly" "Oh ok, I'm originally from Southwest Philly, I've been here since the Reagan administration." "Well, you haven't missed much." My joke landed smoothly as he chuckled and I mentioned that, "It was a great day when Senator Obama paid a visit to our neighborhood during his presidential campaign in 2008." I told him how the city remained on fire when the Phillies also won the World Series that same year. He mentioned a few sports players but I had no clue who they were because of the obvious generation gap. It's always better to actually take the time to get to know someone instead of judging them because of their reputation or current circumstance. That's not cool. I clearly was able to establish trust with Willie as he disclosed. "You know what Cornell, I still love this country and served it proudly for two tours in the seventies before I got arrested. I don't tell folks that because I don't want the stigma of another crazy vet gone mad.

My crimes had nothing to do with the time I spent in the army. I was honorably discharged and I would like for it to stay that way. It's the only thing that's still pure to my heart with the exception of my daughter back home." "Thank you kindly for your services sir." "You're welcome." He then offered me a small box of iced tea and we continued. I then told him of my brief interest in the service, "After graduating high school, I was about to take the ASVAB test to join the Airforce but had a change of heart and decided to attend college." He laughed, then asked, "So you went from college to jail?" "Yup." That's pretty strange but hey, things happen. But I'm glad that I didn't go to college. I would have had a lot more bodies. The judge probably would have given me 300 years. Since they never created the flying cars that everyone thought that they would have by the year 2000, if I'm lucky by the time I go home, there might be an express train that takes you to Mars." He sure made my day with his bright humor and great personality. I was happy that I took the time and got to know the real Willie Beckman. We became close and he always mentioned if I needed anything, just ask or have one of my assistants stop by the inventory room. My case was a done deal, and with being halfway through my sentence, still being a young man with a bright future, the world was still mine. But I knew that the courts made mistakes all the time, so I had a couple of friends from the Law Library look into Willie's case for any loopholes. Willie was thrilled to hear but was also pretty candid. "Cornell, this is a blessing, I should be dead. I passed out after thinking my last victim was dead. She ran away, instead of killing me as I laid unconscious. The judge found it in his heart to give me that crazy sentence, just in case I believe in reincarnation and return to this earth, so I'd still be in prison. For all that I've done, I was still shown mercy. No complaints on my end. I love my LIFE."

CHAPTER 12

Foreign Exchange

RIGHT BEFORE GRADUATING high school, a lot of my friends planned to postpone college to travel the world to see different countries. Kudos to the ones that were able to experience the adventure. It sounded pretty exciting. If I would have opted to study abroad, my choices would have been Brazil, Amsterdam, London, or Greece. Realistically, I would have been a complete failure due to all the distractions. I personally don't know anyone that was a foreign exchange student, but I educated myself that a foreign exchange student is usually a high school or college student, who travels to a foreign country to live with a hosting family and to study abroad, as part of a foreign exchange student program. It's not always the case where the student has to find a counterpart from the other institution with whom to exchange. Exchange students usually live with a host family or a student lodging program. The cost for the program varies by country and institution which are funded by scholarships, loans, or self-funding. The foreign exchange programs simply provide students with an opportunity to study in a different environment and to experience the history and culture. Student exchanges became popular after World War II, and are intended to increase the participant's understanding and tolerance of other cultures, as well as improving their language skills and broadening their social horizons. An exchange student typically stays in the host country for a period of 6 to 10 months.

Some programs allow the student to stay in the country for several years depending on the circumstances. I never saw them around campus. It's not as if they were wearing a huge sign on their backs that read, "Foreign Exchange Student." But I did overhear some of the sorority girls mention how hot some of the guys were that came from France and Germany. Lloyd made a few attempts to hook up with a few Asian girls but I guess his aggressive manner scared them off. The exchange student's success rate, compared to a regular college student, was astounding. According to study abroad. ucmerced.edu, "97% of study abroad students found employment within 12 months of graduation when only 49% of college graduates found employment in the same period. 25% higher starting salaries: that's how much more study abroad students earn than those college graduates who do not study abroad. 90 % of study abroad alumni who applied got into their 1st or 2nd choice of grad school. 80% of abroad students reported that study abroad allowed them to better adapt to a diverse work environment. 70% of study abroad alumni claimed that because of study abroad they were more satisfied with their jobs. With these high success rates, I now have a better understanding of why Vanessa chose to take off to London. Every now and then she would cross my mind. But I was in prison, and she was halfway across the world probably hooking up with some Englishman. But I'm sure everything about being a foreign exchange student wasn't a walk in the park. Like all new experiences, there had to be some pitfalls. I just hope nothing horrendous fell upon Vanessa and that all was well. She was a big girl but some of the horror stories and weirdness that took place overseas caused me to doubt that Vanessa was totally prepared.

Here are a few weird stories from the foreign exchange program. A female student joined a family that lived in Russia. When the student arrived, the family didn't have the money to host the student and the student had to find a job and pay for her own food, which is against the rules. The parents are supposed to provide for all immediate needs because it's supposed to be family-oriented. The parents also had a daughter who was 15, very shallow and obsessed with boys and drinking. After several months, the student had to go back home (Virginia) because of some personal issues, and then when she went back to Russia, she found out that the 15-year-old daughter had stolen a thousand dollars from her credit card which was the entire balance. That was bad, but here's another uncomfortable scenario. A female student joined the exchange program in Central America, she shared a room with her host sister, the sister decided that it was ok to steal clothes, smoke in the room and hide the cigarettes in the student's drawers, then rat her out to the parents. Not cool. The host sister also demanded that the student hang out with her friends but got mad because the student wasn't cool enough like Americans should be. Surprisingly, the host mother got the idea that the student was trying to flirt with her husband and solicit him for sex, which she did not. The mother then blamed the student for her husband going out and getting a mistress. The mother then went to the extreme and contacted the foreign exchange program, demanding that the student be removed from their house and placed elsewhere. Either the student did in fact flirt with the husband and gave the wife a reason to feel uncomfortable or the wife was intimidated as foreign exchange students are well known to be very attractive and exotic looking.

For the next experience, a male student did the program in a small town in eastern Germany. It's not a horror story but clearly explains that weird people do exist all around the world. The student stayed with a very conservative husband and wife. They had no computer and the phone was "very expensive," even with a phone card. The student had trouble reaching his parents for several weeks and of course, got homesick. When the student asked to use the phone, the host's parents told him to have his parents call because it was cheaper, ok understandable. The student walked to a nearby café and sent an email letting his family know that he was ok. The next day the host mom gave him the phone; it was the student's high school German teacher. The teacher asked if he was, ok? Then placed his mom on the phone. Apparently, the student's mom had been trying to call several times and when the host parents heard English or limited German language, they just hung up and didn't say anything to the student, so that's why the student's mom contacted the high school teacher because the host parents kept hanging up on her. The student ended up asking the exchange program about other living arrangements. The program transferred the student to live on his own in a nurse's quarters on the top floor of a creepy but still functional hospital. What the hell? But the student didn't think it was all that bad, there were a couple of French kids also staying there and they had "Krankenhaus Party's." It's basically just a regular party with drinking and dancing. Wow, some experience. Well, they asked for it, they certainly got it. Another unusual situation but more comical is when male student went to Mexico. He explained that the family was always switching around all of the rooms in the house, leaving the student to go track down the kitchen. One week the kitchen would all of a sudden be the living room. This happened every few weeks for the entire year. He eventually thought they were just messing with him and probably still laughing about it until this very day. But it's a great chance that the family probably didn't have the proper vents, so they probably used a powered hotplate and moved it around to prevent the buildup of grease on the roof or walls.

The last tale comes from the parents who had a student stay with them in a small town in South Africa in 2017. This student was a complete idiot. She stole booze and tried to blame it on the maid. She came and went all hours of the night as if she owned the place. The host parents encouraged her to leave where she went to another household where she didn't last long either. The student eventually began spending time with a local obstetrician. She began telling people she wanted to be an obstetrician and that the experience she would be getting would shape her future plans. The doctor was convinced and allowed her to attend live births. She left after a year and the new host parents thought that was the last they would hear of her. Not at all. In February, during the pandemic the FBI showed up in town and questioned the doctor. Turns out the student needed a baby to keep up a lie, so she told her boyfriend who wanted to bolt that she was pregnant. So, she killed some poor woman by skillfully cutting off the umbilical cord and incorrectly removing her baby during birth. That's crazy. But I guess this one did learn something during her stay in South Africa. But one would ask, "Why would some parents even sign up to host a student if you're going to waste time by treating the student poorly?" There are a couple of answers. Some families get a stipend to cover expenses for the guests. Similar to why abusive people foster children, they see them as a paycheck. For others, it seemed to be a fair exchange, the exchange for their child to go to a great school with less cost outside the country.

During the American Revolutionary War (1775-1783), exchanges of prisoners were made in the field or at a higher level of an organization. However, on December 11, 1861, the U.S Congress passed a joint resolution calling on then-President Lincoln to "inaugurate systematic measures for the exchange of prisoners." For example, one private officer was worth another private; corporals and sergeants were worth two privates. Lieutenants were worth three privates and commanding Generals was worth sixty privates. According to en.m.wikipedia.org, "Prisoner exchanges took place after the 1948 Arab-Israeli War when Israel exchanged all its Palestinian prisoners and POWS (Prisoners of War Soldiers) from Arab armies in exchange for all Israeli soldiers and civilians were taken captive during the war. This method is brilliantly portrayed by Tom Hanks in the classic movie "Bridge of Spies," which was released in 2015. Hanks strangely plays the role of an insurance lawyer who negotiates the release of a U.S pilot after his spy plane was shot down during the Cold War. The exchange would take place in Berlin. If all went well, the Russians would get a convicted spy named Rudolf Abel. It was a great movie that went on to be nominated for an Academy Award and won the Academy Award for Best Actress in a Supporting Role. In 2011, a middle east prisoner exchange was maybe less popular to some Americans but certainly interesting as the agreement between Israel and Hamas was for one soldier, in exchange for 1,027 prisoners, who were mainly Palestinians and Arabs-Israelis. Two hundred and eighty of these prisoners were sentenced to life in prison for planning and perpetrating various attacks. The deal was authorized by heads of both countries. In January of 2016, Iran freed four Americans of Iranian descent from prison. It was a delicately negotiated swap with the United States, which in turn released seven Iranians who had been held on sanctions violations. President Obama's administration paused the annoyance between the two countries with this deal that dated all the way back to the late '70s and early '80s during the Iran hostage crisis. Also, in 2016, Cuba and the United States were in discussions of exchanging a prisoner who is considered to be one of the most damaging spies in recent history, said U.S officials. A female prisoner, who was convicted in 2002 for spying for the Cuban government for nearly two decades while working for the U.S Defense Intelligence Agency. She's not bad-looking, and while at the Defense Intelligence Agency, she became the top Cuban analyst. Investigators said she memorized classified information on the job, typed it on a laptop computer in the evenings at her apartment, stored it in coded form on disks, and passed the information to her Cuban handlers. She was sentenced to 25 years in prison and due to be released in 2023. I say, if the U.S. Defense Intelligence Agency was actually that intelligent, they would take her out of lock-up and offer her a damn job. Clearly, she has been doing something right. Most people can't even keep a regular paying job for two years. This woman was able to fool the so-called most powerful country in the world for almost two decades. Not two weeks or two years, ALMOST TWO DECADES. Can you imagine the type of information she obtained during that extensive amount of time? Maybe all sorts of backyard deals made by government officials, people's secret identity to their secret identity, passcodes for our military strategies that could have been leaked to the world's biggest terrorist groups, Isis and Al-Qaeda. She sounds like the female James Bond, and maybe this could be a hint for a pretty good movie in the making. This is one dangerous woman. Never mind her assistants during the two-decade ride, whatever hole they've been hiding in or perhaps have moved on to another client, who probably works as one of our commanding officers in the armed services. But the deal landed smoothly, and the U.S would be getting back Americans who sought refuge in Cuba from U.S prosecution. Federal law enforcement officials are designated to capture these types of criminals. One stated that "Cuba has been a safe haven for U.S. fugitives." U.S officials would like to retrieve a female prisoner, who escaped from a New Jersey prison in 1979 where she was serving a life sentence for killing a state trooper by shooting him with his own gun at a traffic stop.

In 2007, the Taliban said they had killed an Afghan hostage who was the friend of a prisoner that was swapped. There was a journalist that was freed in March of that year from La Repubblica, in exchange for five Taliban fighters released by the Afghan government. Italy supported Afghanistan to make the deal. But the Taliban killed the translator and the driver because they failed to make an additional swap. Overall, most of these cases were due to espionage which also had pretty interesting statistics. 60% of espionage cases began in the United States with a large majority of those on the East Coast. 15% of spies held a top-secret SCI (Secret Compartmentalized Information) clearance at the time they began committing espionage. In 2018, out of the one-hundred and eleven spies who succeeded in passing information to foreign countries, 27% were caught in less than one year. I wasn't really surprised to see that 49% of these people worked in the military. 18% were government civilians, 24% were government contractors, and 9% had already left government service or their job was unrelated to their spying. No surprise that males dominated this profession at 93% and women with the remaining 7%. Furthermore, they weren't the chosen ones by some ancestor family ritual. 64% of these spies took the initiative in volunteering their services to a foreign intelligence provision. Each motive for carrying out such a mission could have been simply because of money, disgruntlement, or revenge toward an employer. Regardless of the high risk of getting caught, some still proceeded in exchange for a local business in their country, a comfortable retirement plan or to help their ailing parents. I also thought the sentencing guidelines for perpetrators were interesting. 18% of the criminals received less than 5 years, 20% received 5 to 10 years, 18% received 10 to 20 years,

10 % received 20 to 30 years, only 2% received 40 years, and 12% received life in prison.

But luckily some had immunity from prosecution or chose to save taxpayers the drama of the legal proceedings and just committed suicide after getting caught.

CHAPTER 13

Mother

MY MOTHER, BEVERLY Anderson did a wonderful job dealing with the many headaches that I inflicted. But on the day that I left for college, she made it clear, "Oh I'm going to miss you giving me such a hard time." But my little sister, Trish was thrilled, "I'm not, can I have his room?" This is probably the most maudlin chapter in the book because it really hits home for mothers who've anticipated the day that their children leave for college after doing extremely well, versus the day that their children leave for prison due to a rebellious lifestyle. The thought is assumingly unsettling when reality settles in that the innocent, adorable child you carried for nine full months will be leaving the nest to sprout their wings, pursuing higher education, or hauled off for exploitation by the criminal justice system. As it was told to me by my Queen after leaving for college. "Cornell, I know that you're a smart kid but I really didn't know where you were, or who you were with. The feeling of the unknown resulted in many sleepless, worrisome nights. I loved seeing your letters in the mail, your name popping up on my cell phone and you coming home for the holidays. The holidays that you missed; I just went to work to keep myself occupied (Mother is a nurse at a local hospital). The feeling of not seeing you each and every day and being restricted for certain times of the year was like dangling a steak in front of a starving dog.

Oh, how I missed you, my beloved son. I missed the irritating loud rap music you often played and you leaving your clothes in the washer and dryer. I hope that you're wearing those headphones I bought you and you're not inconveniencing your roommate with that racket. College is like the street, a good place but you have bad influences."

Her words to me while I was in prison were just as touching. "One day as I came home from work, I anticipated you sneaking one of those fresh girls into your room but after creeping up the steps and opening your door, it was completely clean and quiet. I miss you son. God is the greatest but I cry often at night because I don't know what will become of you after this journey. This system has created a maze for you but please allow God to help navigate you during this time of adversity. Cornell the church is praying for you. You are my son and I will not turn my back on you. I don't care how many women you think loves you, I am the only woman that will love you unconditionally. I also don't care about how many books your instructors are advising you to read, just remember that the Bible is the most important book that you're supposed to study. Once you master that book then it will give you the answers to the rest of the other books. Please keep positive people around you at all times. Jail is like the street, it's a bad place but you have great people such as yourself, trying to better themselves. Your aunt invited me over to her house for a little girl's night out, but I was a complete party pooper. All I kept talking about was Cornell, Cornell, Cornell." Tears gushed while typing my mother's emotions that explained my departure for higher learning and my incarceration to a state penitentiary. Of course, for me the feeling was similar, that's the whole point of me writing this book. When I laid on my bed in college, I felt like I was in jail while staring at the number of F's for my final grades. The feeling of disappointment and being a complete failure was evident.

On a beautiful sunny day in the yard, I expressed concern about Ryan and Justin's parents. "Hey guys, I'm a bit late showing concern but how are your parents holding up?" Ryan explained, "Yeah when the judge read my sentence, my mom said she immediately signed up to join a support group. My father is drinking twice as much because he always pours a glass for me." Justin said, "Yeah, my mom is cool. She's always trying to beat me over the head with the word, but she got a second job, working part-time at the supermarket. The employee discount helps with food since I'm not there to help. She said that she hadn't felt this lonely since I left for college." I replied, "Damn man, we never think about the toll it takes on our parents when we make bad decisions and being around bad company." Ryan added, "It's like they're also incarcerated. All that psychological stress, even when leaving for college." But I admitted, "Bro, I wasn't thinking about how my mom was going to feel, once I left for college, I was thinking about getting into some panties." We all shared a huge laugh from me being candid. On a website called circleofmoms.com, which was created for mothers with children that are incarcerated, one mother confessed to being absolutely fed up that her son has been in and out of prison since he was 13. "The boy has been doing drugs, stealing cars at night, and hanging with the wrong crowd. He's now 19 and heading back to prison. I'm considering not writing to him, not visiting, not sending any money, and just cutting him off completely, just so that he can learn his lesson." She admits that it's just too much to handle as she is currently still in school and working as a nurse.

After venting, the mother gained an ally. "Sometimes it's just best to stop being their lifeline because they will never learn. I'm sick and tired of being the safety net for this grown man, who beat the crap out of my two, previous boyfriends. I'm finally having great sex now, so I told the jail to keep him. Haha." Another mother claimed that the reason why her son went to jail for 6 years was all her fault. She constantly asked, "Where did I go wrong with him?" She was ashamed to ask for help and became very depressed. Another mother admitted, "My 18-year-old daughter is in a great state of confusion. She's been dating two different guys at the same time. One guy has been going back and forth to college and the other guy has been going back and forth to jail. Can you guess which guy my daughter is more in love with? She's more in love with the jailbird. It's disappointing and downright stressful. The jailbird has already knocked up another

17-year-old and I'm afraid my daughter will be next. I've made some poor choices at her age but I'm not looking forward to becoming a grandmother at age 34." When another mother disclosed that her 9-year-old daughter pranked someone, they called the cops and the little girl ended up having to go to jail for 2 years. The mother was devastated but kept working with her daughter and when the little girl returned home, she was a perfect little angel.

Other mothers agreed that when the child is that rebellious and completely out of control, if you're not going to call the cops on them, then simply call upon Jesus to deliver them the right way. Another mother offered a passionate rant. "You women that are talking about giving up on your sons are completely nuts. When my son was seven, he was a complete headache. He just graduated from college, found himself a nice white girl, and got married. They have a family hair salon business and just had their first child together. Was I supposed to give up on him so the system could devour him? I don't care how many times he messed up. The only time I'll stop being there for my son is when I die. You women are crazy. Get the hell off this damn internet and go learn something called loyalty. I wonder what would happen to any of you if God gave up on you? You all need to be quiet and not talk." Another agreed, "Yeah, I don't see myself giving up on my son or my daughter and she's worse than him. She has three different fathers for her three kids and she's been to jail three times. She's on welfare then lied to welfare about not having a job but worked part-time at a fast food restaurant. She then lied to the fast food restaurant about being on welfare. She's pregnant now with twins and asked me for money so she could get an abortion. The abortion cost $450, I told her no. Then a week later, I noticed $475 was missing from my debit card. I'm thinking she probably went to lunch with the extra $25 bucks after getting her procedure done with my money. My son has been to jail once but he learned his lesson after his twelve-year sentence. Luckily, he got his degree before going to jail. He's now a manager for an engineering company and doing well."

I recall my mother mentioning that one week prior to me leaving for college she was in the grocery store going over her normal list of items. Right before she went to the cash register, she finally remembered that I wouldn't be home and happily saved herself sixty dollars worth of food. My fraternity recruited several other members that graduated from college and while hanging out in the yard on a mild evening, I asked them about how their parents felt when leaving for freshman year? One member said, "My parents basically dragged me by the throat and tossed me into the car, then left without giving me a hug as I stood there in the smoke and the car sped off." Another guy said, "My mother turned into a wild party animal, she even got on Social Media and took pictures with all my friends back home. Now that I'm locked up, she's really having a blast because I'll be here for another four years." Another guy stated, "My mom misses me. She's a pediatrician and said that there's a dark-skinned baby boy that reminds her so much of me. She said that one day she tried to intentionally keep him for a much longer visit." Another guy said, "My parents were ecstatic. They said that it felt as if they were in college and throwing parties with the neighbors every other weekend because our neighbor's kids had also just gone off to college. Then they told me to also apply for grad school, so I could stay there and receive my Masters and they would be glad to cover the costs but I clearly screwed that up." It's easy for me to give advice because I'm not a mother but there was a wonderful book written by Melissa T. Shultz called, "From Mom to Me Again: How I Survived My First Empty Nest and Reinvented the Rest of My Life." Ms. Shultz offered a few valuable tips for when your child/ children are leaving the nest for the first time.

1. Plan for your freshman's departure, she urges parents to shift some of their focus back towards themselves and find non-parent ways to enjoy spending their time while kids are still in high school.
2. For most parents the sadness will soon pass, most mothers and fathers had real grief after they dropped their kids off at

college. But nine out of ten moved on from this feeling within a month or two, and much sooner.

3. Be gentle with yourself and acknowledge the big changes in your life, this transition will more than likely take place after the kids have settled.

4. Focus on your family, marriage, and other relationships. Reconnect sexually, spiritually with your partner. Many of the related factors and things in common decrease over the years because of caring for the children.

5. Find ways to communicate, some families keep in touch electronically with text groups or social media. Creating a virtual dinner table where the family dynamics can continue.

Clearly, some of these moms don't need Ms. Shultz's helpful tips and gladly accepted the well-needed vacation from the turmoil of their offspring. I remember the first text message my mother sent confirming her thoughts and support. She admitted, "When you left for college that was a pretty rough day for me. "Well, I didn't want to embarrass you in front of your new friends so I blew my nose once we got back to the car. I just prayed that you still kept the morals and values that you were taught. Since I don't speak with you often, I began to make a list of things that I wanted to discuss but I threw it in the trash. It was boring. When you were packing the last of your belongings, it still felt like a dream, it was unreal because you were just born yesterday. I almost came into your dorm room to clean it for you just to make sure that it was my kind of clean. Cornell, please use a condom if you're going to sleep with any of the nasty little girls. Don't ruin your education and career over a few moments of pleasure. I'm really not that much into sports but I took your place next to Pops, watching the Eagles game. If you need anything just call home, ok son, mommy has your back." At times mother can be a very annoying person. But after hearing other stories of student's parents celebrating their absence, not sending them any money when they left for college or were incarcerated made me appreciate her annoyance. I'm confident that the type of relationship that I have with my mother also exists between other mothers and sons. So this poem expresses our appreciation for all of the annoying but loving mothers.

I stole out of your purse after you took me to church. You were the gift; I was the curse while neglecting yourself, and putting your kids first. Thanks, mom, for keeping calm. You were always there reciting Psalms. Your love and support is more than a million, but I would still be in debt if I gave you a trillion. I would terribly regret, if these words weren't sent. You authored my life, with teachings of love and not offering strife. A young child being provided with knowledge and now a man who's gone off to college. Thanks again mom for the valuable lesson that words have the most lasting impression.

With much Love from your son,
Cornell Richards

CHAPTER 14

Co-Ed

MOTHER'S BIGGEST FEAR of me getting someone pregnant and ruining my career secretly became a reality. One morning as it poured down raining, Vanessa woke me up by kicking me. "Wake up, you need to take me to the abortion clinic before I screw up your life." I gave no reply. I didn't even brush my teeth but quickly got dressed and waited several hours for her procedure to be completed. That was freshman year and one would think I would have learned my lesson. This sort of information certainly disqualifies me from becoming president of the United States. The staff at the abortion clinic began to formally address me, "Mr. Richards back again?" I shamelessly admit that throughout my college days about a dozen women had claimed that I was the father of their unwanted pregnancy and received procedures. The greeting from the staff at the local STD clinic was the same. Lloyd accompanied me there for moral support and found some sort of humor from my discomfort. "They should give you a V.I.P section in the clinic or some type of membership." A mid-age, fat, black nurse then called me in to be examined, and read my chart. "In the past, you've tested positive for Chlamydia, Gonorrhea, Crabs, and Trichomonas. Ok Mr. Richards, drop your pants, and whip it out, you know the drill." I did as she demanded. After she squeezed my penis while gently inserting a small wire with a soft head inside my penis, she continued with her unprofessionalism. "Let's hope you have one of the previously mentioned, if not? You're in big trouble. Have a seat in the waiting room, Mr. Richards, I'll be back in twenty minutes with your results." I wanted to tear this woman's head off but had only myself to blame.

It was the longest twenty minutes of my life as I sat there looking around at the other young people that had the same worrisome look on their faces. Minutes later, an elderly couple came out with the woman storming and swinging her cane. "I'm sick and tired of this Rufus, I've been going through this with you for 45 years. You can't keep your, big, old, ding dong in your pants." We laughed as the old man continued to dodge the blows while the security guard escorted them outside. Moments later, the smile was wiped off my face when the nurse returned and called my name. I already had it made up in my mind that I was going to kill everyone in the facility if this woman told me that I was HIV positive. "Ok Mr. Richards, your test results have arrived," she paused then mentioned, "Mr. Richards you've tested positive for a urinary tract infection. Take these pills, drink plenty of water for the next week to help clean out your system. Have a great day and see you again next time." Smartass, I should have reported her but I was too overjoyed with the grace of God. When returning home, I took the pills and drank plenty of water as the evil nurse instructed. The stinging sensation whenever I urinated was gone and it felt like I had a new penis. About a few weeks later, I continued with the same antics but fortunately, I never contracted anything. This sort of recklessness was only tamed because of the enormous amount of prayers from my mother and as time passed, I began to have a better understanding of why she worried about me so much.

The co-eds in college were pretty cool but some white girls made it known to me that "Sorry, I don't deal with black guys." While walking to class in the courtyard, I overheard two white girls say to their friends, "Yeah a few of them are cute and I'd probably hook up with one but I'm not taking home a black guy. What would my parents think?" Another one stated, "My mom wouldn't care but my dad would kill me." Surprisingly, I heard a black girl say to her friends in the cafeteria,

"Before I left for college, my mom made it clear that I should not bring home a black man. She wants diversity in the family." Vanessa and I had a handful of options but it seemed as though we used each other as a nightcap. Especially one day after she and her sorority sisters spent all day in the urban community handing out hygiene bags and school supplies to the less fortunate. Her sorority sisters also visited the local hospitals and donated toys for the kids that were sick and took pictures with them and read stories. Some of the sorority girls were racist but they continued to do some great things for the Urban Community. Vanessa led the way in the clean-up projects and feeding the homeless in dangerous neighborhoods. Obviously, the sorority girls weren't too biased when it came to getting a few extra credits for their education. Of course, on campus, you had a couple of black, aggressive females, who often boasted about not taking any crap from anyone. They were popular at the parties for starting drama. "Oh, hell no chick, I can't believe you just stepped on my toe and messed up my pedicure. Take it out of your little college fund and give me my money." I'm not sure who was in charge of recruiting but I guess they saw talent behind the madness.

In the co-ed dorms, a number of girls preferred that structure, opposed to an all-female living arrangement. When chatting with other sorority girls, a few admitted, "Girls are so catty and competitive, it's just sickening." "Yeah Cornell, it can get pretty rough living in an all-female dorm," "But I'm pretty sure that's how Cornell and his little friend Lloyd would like it. hahaha," I agreed. "That's fair." Another stated, "I had to get the hell out of there, that's one-hundred and fifty different periods that I had to deal with and I don't want to be looking at anyone else's filth. Every Friday night was movie night in the co-ed dorms. It was basically date night. We were given three options by the entertainment department and had to vote one week in advance by sending an email, indicating our choice. If a certain number of people didn't vote, then the director of the department would choose the movie that featured a small snack. Since I spent all week vandalizing Vanessa's vagina and several others, I was completely exhausted and just chose to relax, kick back and enjoy the chosen film. For others, it was one big make-out party. Lloyd rolled around in a sleeping bag with twin sisters, a group of nerds got a chance to hang out with some of the most beautiful women on the volleyball team, some of the new, young female professors hung out afterward, and loosened up. Movie night was sort of a big deal on campus. We were totally unaware that it was our introductory period to those corporate folks who slaved all week, and partied like it was their last weekend on earth when the clock struck five on a Friday. College has a really weird way of molding you into the social norms and pacifying the aching torcher of the typical nine-to-fiver. But that's what we signed up for; that's a part of the memories being built and relaxing on our downtime while pursuing the road to success.

One day while relaxing with the guys in the study room, it was brought to my attention by C Rome that a phenomenon was emerging. "Hey, Richards looks like you may be having some competition." "How so?" I asked, "There's a female sorority being established on the women's side of the facility. They call themselves S.W.P (Sisters With Power). In prison, the only time we came into contact with the females was during church services but they sat on one side of the Chapel and we sat on the opposite side. Since our Frat Gang had become so popular, I was glad to hear that our trend was being extended. "Hey, I think that's a wonderful idea." The guys all nodded their heads in agreement. The officer further informed us that, "They're led by a woman by the name of Jai Scars." I replied, "Interesting name, what's her story?" Rome answered, "Scars graduated from Brown University with her law degree. The story of her arrest had leaked through the jail that after passing the bar exam, like you, she got a great job offer. But after partying with friends on graduation night, she was driving while completely drunk and recklessly killed an entire family of four on their way from church, in a head-on collision. Her attorney was able to paint a very good picture about her coming from a good family and recent achievements. Luckily, her judge had also graduated from Brown and the prosecutor had also graduated from the same University, so of course, being one of their own, she got a slap on the wrist of a minimum, four-year sentence." Justin was amazed, "Can you believe it? This woman killed four people while driving drunk and received only four years in prison." The officer continued, "She's black and beautiful and speaks very confidently." I never got a chance to meet Jai Scars but I heard all of the great things that she had been doing. Her sorority focused on self-empowerment, women bettering themselves academically, and addressed the sexual violence against female inmates. Scars was indeed doing some great things and moved swiftly by having a meeting with the warden. "Warden, I chose the name Scars so that every day I could be reminded about the people that I scarred for life. I just would like to have the opportunity to offer a great contribution while I'm here." The warden then replied, "I believe there's redemption in you Scars, I truly do. So, your petition is granted." The warden granted her petition to have some female ex-cons return to the facility, once a month to tell their story about returning back to society and becoming successful.

Although we didn't live together for obvious reasons, some female inmates still popped up pregnant in other jails across the nation. According to an article in the NewsOK, a report was made about "the number of sexual violence that was doubled at a correctional facility in Oklahoma City. The 2019 Bureau of Justice Statistics report found 15.3 % of the inmates surveyed at the female facility reported some form of sexual abuse or rape from another inmate. This was the highest in the nation for female inmates." Surviving a sexual attack and trying to get adequate counseling and reproductive medical attention is daunting enough for those in society but for those who are incarcerated, this strain seems to be insurmountable. One alleged victim wrote "I am seven months pregnant and I got pregnant here during a sexual assault. I have been sexually assaulted here numerous times. The jailers here are the ones doing it." The guards have unlimited access to where the prisoners bathe and sleep which causes the likelihood of sexual assault to increase. Putting an exact number of how often women are assaulted in prison is difficult because just like the streets, many of these incidents go unreported. They're kept hidden due to fear of further mistreatment like isolation from a comfort zone in the general population. But many of these women had already experienced some sort of sexual abuse in the past. About 80% have dealt with this traumatizing experience before entering the prison system. According to a 2019, statistic that was provided by the "The Sentencing Project." In 2019 there were 215,332 female inmates in the prison system. Similar to their male counterparts, African American women were in the first place and white women trailed second and were incarcerated 53% less of the time than black women.

The risk of pregnancy as the result of a sexual assault is a major concern for the victims. But obtaining emergency contraception or an abortion, if one desired, may be more difficult for women who are incarcerated. While incarcerated, using emergency contraception is usually not possible. Some health department heads think that the emergency contraception pill should be on every prison's prescription formulary. Similar to the lack of emergency contraception, access to abortions has made its way to the courts. Women do not lose their right to decide to have an abortion just because they are incarcerated. The main issue is, how will the prison accommodate or refuse to accommodate a woman's decision? Some questioned the access of transportation to an off-site medical facility, with a court in Arizona recently ruling that a court order to obtain transportation for an abortion cannot be required but a federal court in Missouri ruled that a prison cannot refuse to pay for the transportation of inmates to receive abortions. Another issue is, Who the hell is paying for this type of service? Are tax-paying pro-life Americans being informed that their tax dollars are being used to fund abortions in prison? Some state prison systems fund abortions, while others have no written policy. Only two states specifically mention sexual assault in their prison abortion policy; Minnesota and Wisconsin allow for government-subsidized abortions when the pregnancy results from a sexual assault. The federal Bureau of Prisons also pays for abortion in the case of sexual assault. In another letter to stop prison rape, a female inmate wrote, "One night some medical staff came to test my urine and asked if I was pregnant? I didn't answer them. That same night, three guards, two females and one male came into my cell, sprayed me in the face with mace. They handcuffed me from behind and said, we hear that you might be pregnant by one of our own. Well, we're going to make sure that you abort. The two females beat me as the male guard stood by and watched for about ten minutes."

Jails usually overflow with dangerous and merciless men who are often charged with brutal crimes against women. But hidden behind these tales of petty thieves, roadside murders, or gang wars committed by men there are some truly ruthless, terrifying, and horrendous crimes committed by downright insane female criminals in human history. Take your pick of who sounds the craziest.

1. Aileen Wuornos was a child abuse survivor who later earned money as a sex worker, she was found guilty for killing 6 men in one year and was executed in Florida in 2002. Her notorious killing spree ended up on the big screen. She claimed her murders were committed as an act of self-defense against men raped or who were attempting to rape her.

2. Maria Swanenberg was born in 1839. She was a Dutch serial killer. She poisoned 102 people with arsenic of which 7 died. She looked after children and people who were sick, but later it became apparent that she was poisoning them all. She died while being locked up in a correctional facility in 1915. If you Google her picture, she looks completely out of her mind.

3. Every boyfriend of Vera Renczi ended up vanishing mysteriously until they were all discovered in her wine cellar. There were 32 male corpses all in a decomposed state. She also murdered her own son Lorenzo when he discovered her crime. She later confessed to each and every murder and spent the remaining of her life in prison, where she eventually died.

4. The Angle of Death, Kristen Gilbert was an American serial killer convicted for three murders and two additional attempts of murder when she was a nurse. She killed her patients by injecting them with epinephrine.

5. This Danish Psycho, Dagmar Overbye woman killed 25 children including her own. She committed horrendous

crimes through drowning, strangling, and even burning children to death in her masonry burner.

6. I call this one, the human-vampire although she already had a nickname. The High Priestess of blood, Magdalena Solis was born in Mexico and came from a poverty-stricken family, and to earn money, she got into prostitution at a very young age. She was a member of a Mexican cult and indulged in human sacrifices, torture and even went as far as drinking the blood of her victims.

7. Another clown, who portrayed a vampire. Elizabeth Bathory was known as the blood countess; she was one of the most ruthless female serial killers ever known. She is believed to have tortured nearly 650 girls, mostly teenage peasants. It is also believed that apart from torturing her servants she also bathes in her victim's blood. Insane!

8. Born in 1894 Leonarda Cianciulli was an Italian serial killer who was convicted for killing three women between 1939-1940. Better known as the "Soap Maker of Correggio." She used the bodies of her victims to make soap and even teacakes which she fed to her guests. She was sentenced to 30 years in prison and three years in a criminal mental asylum. But she escaped the well-deserved sentence by dying in 1970.

9. An easier pill to swallow and known as the "Cocaine Godmother" and the "Black Widow, Griselda Blanco was a drug lord in a Miami based cocaine-drug-network and ordered dozens of murders and violent revenge attacks during the drug wars of Miami. She was assassinated in 2012, in a motorbike drive-by shooting in Columbia.

10. Valerie Solanas was born an American radical feminist and became a figurehead for women's repressed anger. She hated men to such an extent that she even created a manifesto called SCUM which stood for the society for cutting up men. She was arrested after attempting to kill artist Andy Warhol. She died because of pneumonia at age 52.

CHAPTER 15

Music

IN COLLEGE, THE pointless relations were great, the alcohol was soothing but the music was my stress reliever. When my day concluded, I would sometimes ignore Vanessa and Lloyd's phone calls to hang out. Sometimes I just didn't want to be bothered. I would take my shower, relax and completely zone out to the soulful, venom-spitting, '90s sound of Az. His classic debut single "Sugar Hill" stayed on repeat. But 2009 was a great year for Hip Hop. It produced one of the greatest freshman classes of all time with rap superstar Drake leading the way with the most record sales, radio spins, features with other artists, and to date has continued to dominate. J. Cole's relentless bars and catchy hooks kept me consciously aware along with his artistic storytelling. Kendrick Lamar certainly accepted the responsibility of the entire West Coast riding on his shoulders and delivered with millions of records sold and eventually won a Grammy award in 2016 for his album, "To Pimp a Butterfly." All three artists are unique and immensely successful, but what makes them similarly great is how each of them sampled their music from the '90s era. That production sound made them more appealing to the past generations but remained true to their craft and new audience. I always played J. Cole's first album, "Cole World" before an exam. Due to him being a former college student at St. John's University, Cole was clearly more relatable. His debut single "Workout" was a huge party anthem and other tracks reminisced about him growing up in Fayetteville, North Carolina and finally graduating with his Communications degree.

I recall having the most interesting smoke session with Lloyd, Vanessa, and several others. When I walked into Vanessa's dark blue lighted dorm, "The Resistance" from Drake's first album, "Thank me Later," was blasting and everyone was sitting in a circle passing around two smoke bongs. In the circle, the two hostile black girls that usually didn't get along with anyone agreed then admitted. "Oh my gosh, this is my song," "Yeah it's like, I need some loving right now." Two white girls, who were smoking, suddenly began touching me and one of them tried to shove a blue pill down my throat. I declined but she insisted. "Huh, come on Cornell, try something different. You'll love it." It was a Molly pill. I continued to resist. "No thanks, I'm good." One of the black girls was very aggressive, "Well maybe he'll like this" and pushed the white girl out of the way and began performing oral sex on me in front of everyone. Completely shocked, by the time I looked around, Lloyd and Vanessa were kissing and taking each other's clothes off. The white girls then began kissing the other black girl. Maybe I was maturing and God was curving my appetite. It was a very interesting night but I wasn't really impressed with being a part of an orgy. It wasn't quite my thing. When I woke up the next morning, I looked around and thought everyone was gone but Vanessa came to the threshold with some tea and began teasing me. "Hey rookie, did you enjoy yourself last night?" "I guess so." "You should have seen the look on your face when Lloyd and I were kissing." I just rubbed my eyes and tried to gather myself as she continued, "Hey, you aren't catching feelings for me, are you?" "No, no you're cool." "Oh, because last night I was saying to myself, why isn't he paying attention to the girl kissing all over him?" I was a bit upset because truthfully, over the years I had begun to fall in love with Vanessa. I was just confused about us. During this time, I just wasn't ready to settle down. I was immature and I should have come out and told her the truth but I, like many other guys, was being selfish and wanted to have my fun with every other girl until I figured out what I wanted to do with Vanessa.

I was wrong and what I did was hurtful. I sincerely apologize to you and I hope all is well on your end. I'm glad she took off and didn't stay to help me because if I hadn't gone to prison my relationship with the Lord probably wouldn't have been restored.

So, as I continued to lay on the floor, she asked again, "Hey are you sure we're, ok?" I expressed myself, "Ok you could have warned me." She boldly replied, "So, what would you have liked for me to do, create and send a personal invite that I'm going to be sleeping with your friend at my party? It just happened. Lloyd and I didn't plan that. Should I remind you of the time that you slept with one of my sorority sisters and you were so nice enough to give her your jacket because she was cold?" "That sorority sister attacked me." "Yeah, some struggle you put up. You guys screw everything moving, now when the shoe is on the other foot, we're supposed to be mindful of your little feelings. Well, you won't be getting an apology Cornell Richards, and if this is going to be an issue then I guess we can't be friends anymore." "Fine" "Fine." I then stormed out and slammed the door. I was pissed. She was so insensitive. But where is Lloyd? I went up and down the hallways looking for him, so I could pound his face in. Regardless if Vanessa and I were in a committed relationship or not, I wouldn't have done that to him. He wasn't in his dorm, so he had to be in someone's room. But I was still hungover and began to get exhausted. I went home, took a shower, and played Jay-Z's first album "Reasonable Doubt." The therapeutic tracks, "Can't Knock Da Hustle," and "I'm Feeling It," was a reality check. They calmed the wild beast that was raging inside of me. Truthfully, I couldn't be mad at Lloyd, I would have done the same thing. Vanessa was gorgeous and she was my friend. I'm glad that I was unable to find Lloyd that morning because I would have ruined our friendship. But I'm pleased that Mr. Sean Carter created such lyrics which helped me relax and to see the bigger picture. The rain was pouring that morning as I repeated, "I'm feeling it" while still being curious as to where Lloyd could be. I then heard a knock at my door and he barged in with the girls from the party while explaining, "Hey bro, I've been trying to get a hold of you, we left out to go grab some breakfast. Here's your favorite. My place is a mess right now, so we're just going to hang out here for a bit."

Unbelievable, so he screws my girl, then buys me breakfast the next morning. Lloyd was something else. But I just had to chuckle as he remembered my favorite, which was hash browns, turkey bacon, and orange juice. I then sent a text message inviting Vanessa over, to which she replied, "On my way." After her arrival, it was "Easy like Sunday morning," from The Commodores as we all sat and enjoyed a delicious brunch. About a week later, my Alicia keys CD went missing. I certainly envy Swizz Beatz but blessings to their beautiful family. I couldn't think of "No One" but those girls that I let in that morning to have brunch. Alicia Keys is one of the greatest R&B artists of all time. Each and every one of her singles has been complete fire and has gotten me through some days that I doubted if I would make it down the aisle. The more I searched for it the more other things appeared to be missing. I couldn't find my Jamie Fox CDs. "Unpredictable," and "Intuition," were my go-to albums to close the deal whenever I invited girls over to my place. I often told Lloyd, "Listen if you invite a girl over and play Jaime Foxx and nothing happens, something is terribly wrong." I started tearing up my entire apartment looking for my R&B collection but became even more frustrated and thought about the possible loss of my Boyz II Men collection. I remember attempting to lose my virginity to the Boomerang soundtrack. It was certainly going to be the "End of the Road" for whoever stole my CDs. After calming down and rethinking, that's when it hit me that my entire "Best of the '90s R&B collection wasn't stolen. I had placed them on top of my closet in a fireproof case. Luckily, I didn't accuse anyone. Ha!

The radio stations at Coal Township catered to pop and country fans. While I always had a great interest in that culture of music, under the circumstances, it was more forced than welcomed. It was during the cold winter when I first heard Maroon 5's "One More Night." That song always caused an adrenaline rush before I started to get some work done. Although I didn't have any control of the track selection, during those winter evenings my moments of reflection would be graced with the melodic sounds of Ed Sheeran's "The A-Team." I couldn't wait to see the video, which was epic. I actually liked Miley Cyrus's smash hit, "Wrecking Ball." She caused a lot of controversy with her social antics but she knows how to make a hit. Loved it! It was expected that Rap and R&B artists would collaborate to make great music but Katy Perry and Juicy J's "Dark Horse" was an instant classic. Variety was good and colored the atmosphere. But Dexter didn't appreciate my song selection. "Why are you listening to that white boy music?" "Because I like to broaden my horizons, expand my mind, think outside the box, you know, that boring kind of stuff that makes people smarter." "I don't have to listen to that garbage to get smarter, I'll just read a book." "Well clearly that hasn't been working for you very well now, has it?" "What the hell is that supposed to mean?" "Because if you were any smarter or had basic intelligence, you'd know that music also educates you." Furious with my reply, Dexter swung at me and grazed my jaw. I had to restrain him. He continued, "You swear that you know everything." We continued to struggle as I humorously replied, "Yeah I do, I'm the freaking man. I knew that the officers would be walking by our cell to make their rounds, so I just shoved him away.

He then insanely dived into his stockpile of paperwork that was kept in a small box and pulled out a poem. Without hesitation, he went on a rambling tirade about me being an uncle tom. "Dumb ass house nigger, Mr. know it all, go figure. They supply the gun with you pulling the trigger, but against your own kind. You think all is well, and all is fine, as you drink and eat their swine. Dumb nigger, thinking you run the jail until given a reality shock like the third train rail. You're oh so frail. Reality check uncle tom, they'll explode on you like the atomic bomb, leaving no time to call mom. You think you're a chess piece but you're just as foul as the words they speak. Get your mind right boy, you're not the Real McCoy, they'll toss you away, like a broken toy." I had no damn clue where this was coming from but I just carefully watched him for any sudden moves as the officers walked by minutes later. Now I was hesitant to go to sleep, and in fear that this clown might stab me while resting. It was getting extra late and one of my favorite songs, "Dreams" from Fleetwood Mac made me extra drowsy.

This was no way to live. Being the bigger person and apologizing was the obvious solution. It was just really crazy how he pulled out the poem and started bashing me. Clearly, he'd built up some sort of animosity towards me and for whatever reason. I could care less. But it was time for damage control. I slept well that night, but in the morning, as we got dressed for breakfast, I apologized. "Hey bro, my apologies for last night, when I saw that you were irritated with the music, I should have just put on my headphones." He nodded and also apologized, "Yeah man, I'm sorry for putting my hands on you." "It's cool. No worries." I just walked out and didn't even ask him about the poem. I wanted him out of my cell ASAP. I quickly ate breakfast and made my way to see our unit counselor Mr. Smith. On the way, I bumped into Stanley. We had our differences but we were cool. "Hey kid, how's it going?" "Stan, this guy in my cell is a complete nut, he swung at me last night because he didn't like the music that I was playing." Stanley jokingly replied, "Hey, I was about to take a swing at you too, if you kept playing that crap in our cell. Hahaha, only kidding." "Man, this dude has to go." Stanley then advised, "Cornell don't be in a rush to shove people out of your life, you never know why God brought them to you." I wasn't convinced, I still went to see Mr. Smith. "Smith, this guy is an idiot, I want him out." "Sorry kid, the jail is packed, there's nowhere for him to go." "Put him under the jail or on the roof." "Hahaha, come on you're like the president of this place Cornell," "Well I guess that makes you congress." I walked out then traded two packs of Noodles for some new batteries. Dexter wasn't in the cell but I wanted to set the tone that I didn't want to be bothered. American Idol contestant Adam Lambert's "What do you want from me?" was one of my favorite songs. I think he did a pretty good job on the show and should have received more votes. A new pop sensation who had an interesting stage name was certainly getting a lot of airplay and topping the charts with her new single. Lorde's new single "Royals" from her Pure Heroine debut album took some time to grow on me but her second single, "Team" was more to my immediate liking. The beautiful and talented Ellie Goulding became one of my instant favorites when hearing her "Lights" single.

It sounded like something from Michael Jackson's catalog. Her second effort "Burn" was a complete masterpiece.

One song that was strikingly addictive was "Sweater Weather" by The Neighbourhood. I really appreciated their style and added them to a list of new artists to research after returning home. Dexter, now entered the cell and I just closed my eyes and faded away to the extraordinary voice of Adele. Every other station was playing her entire "21" album. "Set fire to the Rain" was and still to this day, is my favorite song from the English Goddess. During college and prison, music was my escape because it immediately whisked me away from reality. It was better than sleep because, with sleep, I had to patiently wait for my body to be exhausted so I could unconsciously travel to a distant place. I had a newfound respect for the radio. Being subjected to such minimal access to exclusive new material held my hand during the humble beginnings. I missed the internet, especially YouTube. The amazement of typing in your favorite song and it magically appearing along with the video seemed like a fairytale when explaining it to those who hadn't seen the streets in the past decade and those who sadly will never see them again. "What the hell is YouTube?" "Hmm... it's a program on your computer that allows you to simply type in any song you want to hear and the video pops up." "Hahaha, get the hell outta here." One guy said while laughing hysterically. He bragged, "Well damn, I've been down since 1992." It also appeared as though that was the last time he brushed his teeth. Telling the older inmates stories about the new generation of technology provided them with a sweet taste of the streets. The quality of the headphones wasn't that great, so I treated myself to a reserve pair to maintain my sanity. I don't know how the others chose to cope during their journey but my music played an essential role in me being successful in both college and prison. Not in this particular order but prayer, writing, and music were my three main keys to keeping me on the right track in prison. I was approaching the final year of my sentence and certainly eager to launch off third base.

CHAPTER 16

Documentation

RYAN AND I got a chance to hear a moving testimony in the church from Sorority Leader, Jai Scars. She spoke about her parents not wanting to sign the FAFSA forms so she could get financial aid and the horrifying things she had to do in order to pay her tuition. "I solicited police officers and the security guards on campus for sex. This was my insurance policy for more safety instead of dealing with strangers on the street. I slept with the cook from the cafeteria so I wouldn't have to pay for my meals and he would provide me with the leftovers instead of throwing away all that unpurchased food. My parents wouldn't give me their tax information, so I had to file as an independent student. It was a very bad time for me but I managed to graduate Magna Cum laude. Glory to God." I heard about this issue of some parents not wanting to sign the forms so that their child could further their education. Personally, I never knew anyone who had this issue but my thoughts varied. Maybe the parent was jealous that the child had surpassed their expectations with more opportunities to excel. Maybe the child was a big screw-up and indecisive about his or her future, leaving the parent in fear of shoving thousands down the toilet. Some parents just feel uncomfortable discussing their finances with their children. Several hundred of these cases are seen every year by the financial aid office at well-known universities. Some parents don't believe they can or should contribute, or maybe just simply don't like a particular college. A parent might refuse to take responsibility for the education of a child from a previous marriage. An 18-year-old may be an adult in most states, but for financial aid purposes, students aren't independent until age 24. But without a parent's financial information a student will not be eligible for need-based institutional aid or a Stafford Loan which ranges from $5,500 to $7,500 and up. If the parent can report low income, then a student could get enough aid to cover most of the college costs.

In some cases, parents could make six figures, and if the child is applying to a $50,000 a year college, the student will still qualify for some aid. But independent students have a better shot at aid. That's because colleges determine how much to award based on the student's wages, not a parent's, which almost certainly would be higher. To be classified as an independent student, one would have to check "Yes" on these scenarios and be able to prove it with the proper documentation; over 24 years old, supporting a dependent, married, in the military or a veteran, in foster care, a ward of the state, an orphan or homeless. Proving this status can be pretty arduous. It also requires police records and medical reports showing abuse or evidence that parents are dead, in jail or in rehab as well as letters from teachers and friends who can corroborate the student's story. But ultimately, the financial aid system is not on the student's side if parents simply decide not to fill out the FAFSA form. It really puts the student in a difficult position and the options aren't really good. After the church service, the female inmates were told to leave out first. I stood a fair distance but I could see and hear a few women patting Jai on the back and thanking her for her testimony. "Wow that was great," "Thank you so much for sharing." Ryan had a much better sense of this issue as we exited the church. "Yeah, I can certainly relate to Jai's testimony." "What, you had sex for money to pay for your college tuition haha?" "No, you goof, my old man took out something called a PLUS loan.

Since he was my co-signer, he got burned pretty bad when I defaulted on the loans. His tax returns were seized and they started screwing with his social security payments. He tried to escape the debt by applying for bankruptcy but they just tagged on all sorts of fees and charges for late-payments and collections." "Damn" "Yeah, it was bad, they even snatched the couple of bucks that he had in his savings account." "That's crazy." "We would argue for months. It hurt me pretty bad when he said," "I wish I'd never signed those stupid papers in the first place. You've got a degree but where am I going to live? Because you know that they'll probably come for the house next. Damn sharks." "That's when I got into money laundering and took care of all the bills." "Bro, that's crazy, I think I owe somewhere around $20,000." "That's not bad." "That's terrible, the government should be paying college graduates money, not the other way around. Why should college kids and their parents be in debt after graduation? It's just insane for med students to owe over a hundred thousand dollars just to be qualified to save lives. Why are college kids paying money in order to be productive in the society that they're going to be living in? The government has the money. The same two trillion dollars that was used to fund the war in Afghanistan, can be used to fund our education for free." However, we've seen most recently in 2019 that some celebrity parents will go to the extreme to pay for their children to attend college even if the child did not earn the right to attend a prestigious university. But some local parents were pretty stern when it came to paying for their children's college tuition. In an online article, one dad wrote, "The youngsters today expect everything and cry if they don't get it. I expect my children to pay for their own college just like I did. Suck it up babies, you are not getting a free ride to college, you will actually need to work your way through. Work, what a concept, you don't know what that means yet, but you will learn. And if you are paying for the books and the tuition, maybe you will realize that spending hard-earned money on beer and parties isn't smart." LOL!

Personally, I'm not 100% against this parent's argument. Kids need to learn the value of hard work. But a parent needs to know their child's strength. If a child has a short attention span, then adding an extra workload decreases the child's chances of success. However, here's a wonderful alternative. I remember when graduating from high school, some students bragged about going to a community college. Being a new high school graduate, my ego was on top of the world and I felt as though a community college was beneath the gum under my shoe. My views have dramatically changed. I strongly encourage students to attend their local community college. The expense is feasible as to where the student could pay their own tuition while working part-time. Financial aid is still available along with a payment plan. After graduating, the courses are transferable to the university of the student's choice. Just be sure to meet with the admissions counselor or the individual in charge of reviewing the transcripts to confirm which credits are acceptable if not all. This route is exceptional in minimizing the drama between parents and children that constantly dispute over tax forms. Normally, by the time a kid reaches college, they want their own independence, so a community college is an excellent way to still hold their hand while guiding them in the right direction. Finally, after the student eventually graduates from his or her chosen university, the student's final debt will be radically reduced due to attending a community college. But I ponder on the thought of those parents refusing to help, due to pure selfishness. The day might arrive when you pay the doctor a visit and a kidney or some other transplant is needed, and the child that was deprived is the only one that can save your life. Let's see if the child exercises his or her right of a little payback.

We were in the yard hanging out on a brisk, gray day when Justin reminisced about his mother not wanting to sign and pay his bail release after numerous run-ins with the law. "Bro, I was a knucklehead. I beat a grand theft charge, mom was there, burglary, mom was there, gun charge, mom was there. All that time and money, she got fed up. Enough is enough. She pulled the plug. I'm on my own now. Well, at least I used to be. Thanks, Cornell, for allowing me to be a part of the fraternity. If it wasn't for you, I would be starving in here." "No worries, I got you." Another fraternity member admitted, "The day I stole from my mom was the day she cut ties with me. I was 16, always in and out of jail. I'm 22 now." I then recalled, "My grandfather is old school. He always said, "If you can't hear, you'll feel." Another member confirmed, "So my grandparents, Pop-Pop said that they didn't retire to keep paying my bail. Talk about teaching me a lesson. Where I'm from, you can stand behind the bars and see who's coming in the precinct to pay your bail and they can also see you. When I caught my last drug case, my grandpa came down to pay my bail. I was so happy to see him. When they gave him the release form, he took it, ripped it up into little pieces, and tossed it up in the air like LeBron James used to do with the powder before a basketball game." It was funny, we all laughed but as I completed my last set of crunches, I said, "You know, you can't really blame them for pulling the plug, especially if they gave us chance after chance after chance. I asked the group, "How many chances would you give your girl if she kept cheating on you?" One guy said, "If my girl cheated on me, she wouldn't get another chance to cheat on anybody else."

The remainder of the group laughed and said "No more chances." "That's my point, it's the same thing as it relates to relationships, some of us burnt our bridges and some are still lucky to have that support from our mothers or other family members." Another member who spoke with a southern accent chimed in after doing a set of dips. "I thought my mom was bluffing when she said that she was getting sick and tired of me. She gave up on me but my stepfather gave me a chance. That's all I needed because once he put the house up in order to pay my bail, poof, I took off. Made it all the way across the state and my auntie told on me." It began to rain and we were called inside by the sound of the yard horn. What a coincidence that Stanley gave me the newspaper with the headlines reading, "Tough Love." It was a story about a father refusing to pay his 40-year-old son's bail. The father simply was trying to teach his son a lesson and encouraging him to get his act together after the son was struggling with drug addiction and was arrested for stealing a manhole cover from an Oceanside parking lot. He was charged with petit larceny. Apparently, the son told the guards that he had a medical condition and was experiencing pain and swelling in his hands, chest, and neck but was ignored. They actually gave him Benadryl but that didn't work. The family knew something was wrong when the son didn't call home at his usual 6:30

pm time but of course, didn't know the severity. The mother then got a phone call saying, "Your son expired, for more information, call the local medical center," then the person coldly hung up the phone. The father said that over the month-and-a-half of incarceration, the tough love seemed to be working. The son was clean and sober and talking about putting his life back together after his previous arrest for forging an oxycodone prescription and struggling with an opiate addiction. It's really sad because the son had a 10-year-old little boy and a 12-year-old daughter. Reading this article just made me more thankful that I have parents and a God who never gave up on me.

Another article stated how a 36-year-old mother refused to sign the release forms for her 17-year-old mentally ill son. When he eventually got out on the signature of another family member, he beat the mother then called the cops and told them that he was being abused, and the police put the mother in jail. She was found guilty of child abuse and lost her job as a nursing assistant, which she was employed for twelve years. That was terrible and made me think how some people's kind hearts can lead them down a gory path. The woman rightfully appealed the decision and stated in the article that "I wouldn't have done anything differently. My son needs help and he should not be amongst society. The courts are so stupid that if he beat his own mother, what do you think he'll do if a stranger accidentally steps on his shoe?" The woman also mentioned that "I have another son who's 15-years-old. He's not mentally ill, but if he gets locked up, I'm not going to get him. So, he chooses his friends and whereabouts wisely. I live paycheck to paycheck and have rent to pay, and now I lost my job because of one fool, so now I really don't have the money to bail anyone out." She then concluded by acknowledging the process, "But I'm thankful for an appeals process because the courts certainly got this one wrong. I need my job back so I can take care of my family and God's willing my son if he's willing to accept the help?" Lawyer fees, restitution that may have to be paid after release, a treatment that the courts may recommend that the child has to take. This ordeal can get pretty pricey, so I can understand where a parent is coming from and not wanting to deal with these matters. A few months later, I read in the paper that her appeal was granted and she won her case.

To hell with a damn lesson. Every time I got locked up my mom came and got me to prevent any garbage from happening to me. My parents are Godly people so they allowed God to deal with my wrongdoings, not man. Some may say that I was spoiled, and should have been left to fend for myself because my mother bailed me out during my time of need while questioning my ability to cope with adult life. Some believe parents who behave like this generally don't realize they are doing anything wrong. They think they're showing love to their children. They'll continue to give advice such as, "Loving your children isn't about saying yes all the time or diving in and rescuing them every time they get in trouble. Sometimes you have to be cruel to be kind." I'm against being cruel, I can be stern and be in the middle with my authority but cruel is extreme and borderline abusive. These authoritarian parents with this mindset are adamant that leaving their kids to sink or swim helps them to develop resilience, resourcefulness, and a sense of responsibility which are all essential skills for adult life. Now there are even some full-grown adults that may be lacking in this department. This constant "Fix it now" approach is raising a bunch of spoiled brats who at the first sign of any distress, call their parents to save them from facing their consequences. Saving is easy, quick, and gets the job done. For some parents saving the child makes the parent feel good; it makes the parent feel needed and maybe a little less guilty. But it doesn't help the child grow into strong, independent adults. I don't want to stray too far off the topic but I would like to add that a lot of this parenting philosophy has to do with cultural differences. My statements are not intended to be stereotypical but Americans are more geared towards kicking their children out of the house once the children are 18-21 years of age. In the Caribbean, Asian, and Middle East culture that is not the norm. Children usually stay with their parents until they are married or perhaps after graduating college and move out on their own. In the Asian culture, children cater to their grandparents where the respect level is monumental.

CHAPTER 17

The Staff Member

IN COLLEGE, THE library was mainly filled with students studying pre-law. After the huge traffic of students slowed down, I would watch the students work vigorously in order to meet deadlines. Sarah and Brad, two white intern students, were working on a case before officially being hired by the public defender's office. They were always the first students in the library and the last ones to leave out. One evening after showing me his ID, I teased Brad. "Another day at the office?" He replied with a smile then stated, "Yeah, it always seems that the silly cases are hardest to prove and the tough cases are easier to figure out." "What's this case about?" I asked. "A bull crap robbery for a cellphone. Some guy had an argument with his girlfriend. He cheated on her and she said he took her phone." "Clearly she's pissed, but hope all goes well with this one." "Thanks." Sarah finally arrived struggling to carry her books and fixing her crooked glasses. She looked like a nerdy Mila Kunis. I didn't force her to pull out her ID as she mentioned to Brad, "Hey I got some new info on the case." He anxiously replied, "Ok let's get to work." It was a late Friday evening, no one else was coming into the library, so I decided to hang out with Brad and Sarah and offered some assistance. "Hey, if you guys need an extra hand? I'm here." Brad was thrilled. "Hey, sure thanks, Cornell." Sarah then stated the facts,

"So if someone removes an object from a person's body it's either Robbery or Theft, in this case, the guy was weirdly charged with robbing his own girlfriend during an altercation." I replied, "That's crazy." Brad then stated, "He was never found with any stolen goods but a police officer witnessed a struggle then the boyfriend took off running and was apprehended a few months later at his home. Overall, it's basically, he say, she say, garbage but we'll still have to give the facts to the lead attorney."

I asked, "Could you guys request for the lawyer to push for the case to be dismissed based on malicious intent from the plaintiff because she's just pissed at the boyfriend?" "Sarah answered, "That would be a great option. However, the boyfriend unknowingly committed an error, "He thought that it would be ok, to contact the girl and voluntarily left a message on her voicemail, asking her not to appear in court. He didn't threaten her but he asked her to drop the charges and to tell the judge that all was well. The stupid bitch then gave the message to the police, and the guy was charged with Witness Intimidation." I was amazed, "Wow." Sarah continued, "So he has three charges, "Robbery, Simple Assault, and Intimidation of a Witness." I replied, "I'm sure that I'm not the only one who thought Intimidation of a Witness was if the guy had said, if you come to court, I'll have you thrown off a bridge or chop up your family members and mail them to you in a box. Where I'm from, that's Intimidation of a Witness." Sarah agreed, "Yeah it's pretty silly." I admitted, "But I'm afraid this guy is in a pretty tough spot. With the cop being a witness and the phone call, it's not looking good." Brad agreed, "Yeah we really don't have much to work with and we can't keep offering, she's doing this because she's upset." We all got pretty hungry, so we went across the street to a bar and grabbed a few drinks and something to eat. The bar was packed so we grabbed a table and our fish and chips arrived almost immediately. I then asked, "So, you guys will try and get him a good deal?" Sarah was confident, "Oh yeah for sure, the prosecutor was willing to drop the Robbery and Simple Assault and just hit him with the Intimidation of a Witness, which carries 18 months in a state facility. But the defendant turned down the deal." I was surprised, "Damn, 18-months upstate for a phone call? Hell no, I would've turned it down too." Brad added, "Yeah, that's still a bit much and the guy has no prior convictions." Sarah then became a bit blunt. "You guys, stick your business in the dirt and sure know how to piss off the wrong ones." I admitted, "That's true, but the courts are supposed to see through this garbage. The police report said that this guy ran away, so obviously, he doesn't want any trouble. It doesn't say anything about the guy beating her half to death. If so? I'm sure the photos would have surfaced by now. Since the woman is being emotional the lawyer should be able to gain the jury's sympathy." Brad agreed, "That would be great but the defendant committed another error. He selected a judge trial instead of a jury, which I think was completely stupid and our lawyer isn't the brightest bulb in the room." Sarah stated, "But the judge on this case is a pretty fair and respected judge, he can smell garbage from a mile away." When we returned, there were a few students waiting to get in the library as a few hours remained until closing time. When I returned to the table, Brad mentioned, "Ok we have a couple of days before the trial, so let's just prepare to first ask the prosecutors for a much better deal due to the fact that our guy doesn't have any previous, criminal history. If they refuse, we'll have to prepare our incompetent lawyer to go to war with minimal ammunition."

This case was intriguing and I was curious about the outcome, so I asked, "What day is the trial?" Brad answered, "It's Wednesday at 9 am but probably won't start until 10 am." "Ok cool, I probably won't feel like learning anything on that day, so I'll attend the trial, just to see what happens," Sarah replied and became flirtatious as Brad excused himself to the bathroom. "I gotta take a leak." "Hey Cornell, thanks for all your input, and it would be nice if you could see us in action." I humorously replied, "See you in action by simply handing the lawyer the files with nothing in it." We laughed, then she gave me a long seductive look that was cut short by Brad's return. "Ok, where were we?" he asked. I chuckled then confirmed, "Hey, I'll see you guys in court." I forgot to set my alarm clock for that Wednesday morning but luckily Lloyd called and asked me for the address to the health clinic. "Hey man, my stick is on fire, I need to get to the clinic ASAP." "It's on the corner of 6th and Maine but I have to be in court pretty soon." He replied, "It's cool, this chick is going with me." "Ok cool, see you later." I quickly showered, threw on my ripped jeans and sweatshirt then got to the courthouse by 10:15 am. The proceedings were just underway. Sarah smiled and waved at me. The Defense Attorney was fat, bald, and looked like an untrustworthy, used car salesman. He also was coughing and hacking and just did a poor job, presenting the case. If I was the judge, I would not believe a word out of his mouth. The defendant was poised but certainly doomed as the young, energetic white prosecutor portrayed a thirsty wolf in a search of blood. When the plaintiff was called, you could instantly tell that she was a deceitful, bitter witch, seeking vengeance, and was coached before taking the stand.

But we weren't surprised when the so-called, fair judge was easily manipulated and found the defendant guilty of all charges. What was most surprising was that the judge still gave the defendant an 18-month sentence for all three convictions when the prosecutor offered the same 18-month deal. After the trial, I met Brad and Sarah in the hallway, and Brad admitted, "Well, I guess the 18-month offer wasn't so bad, at least the defendant would have had the felony dropped which was the worst of all three." Sarah agreed, "Yeah, but he still got jerked pretty bad." We then saw the defendant immediately being handcuffed then taken away by the sheriff's department. It wasn't a cause to celebrate but later that night Sarah handcuffed me up to her bed.

After meeting Willie Beckman, the inmate, who had 106 years in prison, I held him to his word and always went to the inventory room whenever I needed something. It was information about Willie's case that was most significant. I wasn't God and certainly made no promises but I informed Willie that, "Man, I think you deserve another chance at freedom. I'll have my guys in the Law Library take a look at your case to try and find some loopholes. It's been years since you've been here but those guys are geniuses, if they find something, they'll file the necessary paperwork to get you a new trial." He was grateful, "Thank you Cornell for even considering such a deed, what a kind heart you have son." In the study room, Ryan rounded up a few jail-house lawyers from our fraternity that would certainly put their best foot forward while working on Willie's case. "Ok boys, gather around, it seems old man Beckman from inventory, has struck a soft spot on our leader the great Cornelius here, so we're presented with the big fossil case to free the old geezer." Everyone laughed then immediately got to work. Ryan pulled me aside and asked, "So what do you think his chances are?" I confidently replied, "You know if the criminal justice system wasn't so terribly flawed and if these guys weren't so good, then I would be more concerned but I'm betting it's a 60% chance that he gets out." My guys had a one-week cut-off period for when they would stop working on a case. Due to so many other cases, they had to work on for FREE, that time period was respectable. After day two, Irish and Gilligan, two young white guys who were in the midst of their 10-year sentences, reported back. Gilligan, spoke confidently in his native Australian accent, "Cornell, it's not looking good, we haven't found a bloody thing mate." Irish assured, and mentioned in his Ireland accent, "But it's still a little early, we'll keep searching." Ryan and I just continued to help the other inmates with preparing for exams but anxiously awaited any news.

On day four, I visited with Willie again. "Hey kid, how's it looking?" "Not good Willie, it's day four and my guys haven't found anything but it's an entire one-week process, so you have a couple more days. Something is bound to pop up that has merit for a new trial. On day six, I walked to the study room with Ryan and Justin. Ryan seemed to be losing heart and said, "Man, we've had the hot hand until this case." As soon as we entered the room Gilligan wasted no time informing me. "We thought we'd found something but nothing Cornell." I then issued a few words of encouragement, "Ok men, great job, keep fighting." We now had just one more day and the window was closing. That night in the yard, as I myself began to lose hope, it was Justin that comforted me by reminding me of our fallen fraternity brother Nate. "You know Nate's watching, you know he's pushing for us." "Yeah well, we sure need Nate to send down some angels to help us because we need them right about now. I'm the last hope for the old man." I hadn't really accepted defeat, I really just accepted the reality that this guy had dug himself a hole and no matter how big my heart was, no matter how hard my guys worked on his case, there was absolutely nothing we could do. The next and final day, Irish and Gilligan washed their hands with the case after working all day. Gilligan was remorseful, "Cornell we're really sorry, but we found no merit to issue documents for a new trial." Irish conceded, "It's unfortunate but we have to move on." That day in the study room I just stood scratching my head and rubbing the bridge of my nose in frustration. It didn't feel right, something else had to be done. I know that the guys worked pretty hard on the case and as expected, the week went by in a flash but it just felt as though a lifeline was heading my way. But it was in fact day seven, so I had to break the news to Willie. "Hey sorry they didn't find anything." He was heartbroken. "Huh man, well at least they tried, tell them I said thank you. I'll be sure to send up some extra blankets and hats and gloves for their hard work." I happily replied, "Hold on to those hats and gloves young man, I've got a plan." I then took off, with him yelling, "Well at least tell me something." I actually had two plans. I knew that my fraternity lacked material when working on Willie's case but I remembered that Brad and Sarah worked for the Public Defender's office back home. Maybe I could reach out to them for some assistance, so I wrote them a letter. My second bright idea was to simply ask Irish and Gilligan for an extension. One of these plans had to come through. I was actually more geared towards getting the extension. "Come on guys, I know it's a bit much to ask, and maybe a bit selfish towards the other inmates but this guy really deserves another shot. I'll even purchase you both twenty dollars worth of groceries as an incentive. That's a lot of food." They both looked at each other and agreed. Gilligan said, "Ok, one more week but we'll have to start next week." I quickly reported back to Willie, "Hey Willie, I got us an extension and the guys will be going back to work on the case," "Cornell, God bless you, your efforts are remarkable."

A week later, I received a letter from the Public Defender's Office and I was filled with excitement that they replied so quickly. Surprisingly, the letter mentioned that Brad and Sarah had gotten married and started their own firm as prosecutors and wished me good luck in my endeavors. This information certainly wasn't going to help me, damn traitors. It appeared to be a deja vu all over again with zero findings for the first two days. Irish informed, "Nope, nothing yet." By the time day four rolled around, it was a real nail-biter but I was less stressed. I had finally come to the realization that I've done everything humanly possible to help this person, who might go back out there and kill some more people or enjoy his golden years as a free man. Day five was the same result. While typing on the computer, Gilligan just shook his head and said, "Nope nothing." On day six, I was pretty much exhausted and wasn't really expecting much of a change. I had slept in for breakfast and lunch and was still tired when strolling into the study room late in the afternoon. Gilligan greeted me with a smile then said, "Bingo mate, we got something, as a matter of fact, we have a couple of things." "Irish explained while smacking on his fruit snacks that I ordered for him. "The first card we can play is there were no warrants to search his home where they found all of the weapons. They convicted him on suspicion of murder because of the blood trails, but they never found the bodies. The only thing they have is the rape and attempted murder of his last victim who escaped but he already served that sentence. So, we'll issue the documents for a new trial and request for time served." I explained this to Willie and he almost fainted. "The guys found merit in issuing the documents for a new trial." "Thank you, thank you, Cornell." Three months later, Willie got a response from the courts, issuing him a new trial. He was granted time served and released after 43-years of incarceration. On the day he was released, Ryan and I just watched him through the gates hug his daughter after she arrived to pick him up. Willie is now receiving his veteran's benefits.

CHAPTER 18

Rome Burns

LATE IN THE afternoon Ryan was relaxing on the unit and overheard two officers boasting, "Boy, that Cornell Richards guy is the man. He's screwing the warden. I thought it was a myth but Rome escorts him over to the admin building at least twice a week." "No way" "Yup she's the one who got Richards that 65-inch television." Ryan instantly felt betrayed and came over to the study room and confronted me as I sat with the other fraternity members. "Cornell, what the hell is going on?" I looked confused, then asked, "What are you talking about?" "I just heard from two officers that you're screwing the warden." I just sat there speechless. Justin asked, "Cornell is that true?" I was guilty, but why the hell did Ryan have to expose me in front of everyone? The rumor quickly spread like a wildfire and split my fraternity in half with some applauding me and others feeling betrayed. Justin kept his distance but the officers congratulated me with one saying, "Well I'm glad someone was able to get to her. Now she probably won't be such a total bitch." Overall, my popularity had grown and I was well respected throughout the facility but I felt terrible about tainting our struggle. I had lost a friend with Nate, now I had lost great comrades with Ryan and Justin, who remained giving me the silent treatment. When I bumped into Mr. Phelps he asked, "So how was it when you banged the warden? From the minute, I heard I knew it was true." I quickly replied with a smile, "No comment." "Oh, come on, don't give me that evasive corporate bull crap answer." I just walked away while smiling. I understand how the fraternity felt, but how many of them would have passed on the chance if the same opportunity fell on their lap? However, my actions were a total distraction. We were supposed to be recruiting gang members and helping them to make the transition to college life but now folks were just inquiring about how to socialize with girls.

Some space was needed between me and the guys, so during the day I just chilled out in my cell or read the newspaper on the unit. As I turned the pages, an officer apologized for interrupting me. "Sorry to bother you Mr. Richards but the warden wants to see you." It was a beautiful sunny day but slightly chilly as we walked through the campus. I feared this meeting with the warden wouldn't go as usual because the rumor of our affair must have gotten back to her. Once I closed the door behind me, she snapped. "You just couldn't keep your damn mouth shut, could you?" I explained, "It wasn't me. One of my guys overheard some officers chatting." She believed me and replied, "Ok, I can easily have a group of Bloods stab all of them." Shocked at her response, I instantly remembered that they never found out who killed Nate but it now came clear that it was the warden who had Nate killed by the Bloods. She had indirectly spilled the beans due to panic and frustration. I wanted to tear her pretty little face off but I remained calm. She then brushed me away like a dirty peasant. "Just go, just go, get the hell out of my sight." The officer attempted to escort me back to the unit but I informed him that I needed to get back to the study room. "Hey officer, I think that I might be needed in the study room, so you don't have to walk me all the way across campus." "Are you sure?" "Yeah, I'm good."

When I saw Ryan, he tried to give me the cold shoulder but I firmly mentioned, "Look we have a situation." Justin was concerned, "What's wrong Cornell?" I didn't hesitate, but lowered my voice and explained, "Look, I know you guys are still pissed at me but I just found out that it was the warden who had Nate killed. She just flipped out on me after thinking I told the entire jail about us.

I honestly told her that it wasn't me and that it was one of my guys who simply overheard some officers chatting and then she threatened to have you and the officers stabbed. We have to get her out of here before something happens to one of us or the guards." Ryan remained pissed, "See, you should have never started with this woman." I replied firmly, "If I never started with her then I probably wouldn't have found out who killed Nate, now let's team back up and focus on the bigger picture here." "Justin agreed, "Yeah but we have to act fast." Another one of our members boldly stated, "Cornell, me and Chino here will be here long after you're gone and if you're talking about bringing down the warden, you're going to need a lot of help." Chino was a huge, muscular-built, Puerto Rican guy with his face covered in tattoos. He also didn't like officer Benson very much, the officer who gave me the write-up for breaking the razor. Chino then confirmed his excitement, "Yes, I finally get a chance to smash that clown. Just say when Cornell." Chino was willing to sacrifice himself by intentionally beating up Benson which would result in Chino being sent to solitary confinement and the jail would immediately be placed on lockdown. I would now have enough time to write another proposal to the state, requesting for them to put the warden under investigation for murder. I went to the door and saw Benson relieving the on-duty officer. I waited patiently until Benson was by himself. We wouldn't have a lot of time as the other officers would be making their rounds to check on the study room. But when Benson was finally alone, I unleashed Chino. "Ok, go"

Chino perforated Benson's face and dragged him across the floor like a rag doll while the other guy grabbed the radio and called, "Officer down, officer down in the study room hallway." Everyone else including Ms. Foley stood in amazement. But I think Chino really overdid it as the beating continued, and left Benson in a pool of blood. About ten officers arrived and Chino submitted by kneeling and placing his hands behind his head. The jail was immediately placed on lockdown for the next two weeks and that was more than enough time for me to write my letter to the state, requesting for the warden to be investigated for having Nate murdered. Those two weeks were very trying times. Dexter became more annoying each day along with my workout sessions being postponed. I still felt bad for Chino but felt even worse when Benson finally returned and did his rounds a few days later with two black eyes and the stitches remaining in his lips. He looked terrible but God really hates ugly. A confirmation letter was sent to me, informing me that my document was under review. Right before the two weeks had finally ended, we received new inmate handbooks. When I opened it, the position for warden was vacant. The horns rang and the announcement was made for "All normal activity to continue throughout the prison." Everyone was so relieved. The majority of inmates ran directly to the showers to bathe their salted skin while others immediately jumped in front of the television like an obsessed woman that missed her soap operas. I couldn't wait to see Ryan and Justin. After my 45-minute shower, I got dressed and headed to the cafeteria. I told the server, "Please load me up, I don't care what's on the menu." "Gotcha Cornell." After feeding my face with two turkey sandwiches, chicken soup, and peaches for dessert. I went to the study room where Ryan and Justin sat with poker faces. I thought they would seem more thrilled about our victory but they had plans for me. I greeted them, "Glad to see your ugly mugs." Justin stuttered, "Cornell, I think I'm going to do my own thing from now on." I was confused, and asked, "What do you mean?" "This was great man, but I just want to branch off and create my own fraternity here. Ryan chimed in, "Yeah, I think that would be best for everyone. We accomplished a lot together and I think starting my own fraternity would be a pretty good idea as well." Shocked, I just replied, "Ok cool, totally understandable. So, what did you have in mind for your fraternity Ryan?" He confidentially replied, "Since I'm educating people, I don't think you should have to use profanity even when making valid points. So, I'm starting a Christian fraternity. Instead of waiting to hear the word only on Sundays, guys can meet here for a bible study or for personal sharing of wanting to dedicate their life to Christ. I'll call the fraternity, The Devoters." I nodded my head in agreement, then stated, "Yeah that's a great idea, Ryan, that's surely needed." I then asked, "So what did you have in my mind, Justin?" He was excited to share, "Man, take a look around, everyone is eating garbage, either it's served to us or we're ordering it off the commissary list. I've decided to start a better diet fraternity called Starvers because we're going to be excited and starving for better health. I did a little research and 20% of inmates who are incarcerated for more than 10 years, return back to society with either high blood pressure or diabetes. So, the fraternity focuses on better eating habits and collaborates with The Devoters twice a week to receive the word, so we can have a full pure cleanse." At first, I was upset but after they explained, both fraternities sounded like they would eventually take over the prison. I was impressed. Ryan stated, "Look, Justin and I just got hit with an additional year after seeing the parole board. We know that you have a parole hearing coming up in the next few months, so either you can choose a successor before you leave or we can choose someone to take over Frat Gang after you're gone." I really felt bad for them. "I'm sorry to hear about you both being denied parole."

Ryan sadly replied, "It's cool, as long as there's a parole date set for me, I'm good." Justin joked, "Yeah, compared to some of the other guys we're already on the street, even if we had five extra years." Ryan asked, "So what's it going to be, do you have anyone in mind that you would like to take your place, Cornell?" "Yeah, maybe my cellmate Dexter or I'll pick someone else from the fraternity." That night as I laid in my bed, Dexter was up listening to my radio with the headsets. I was supposed to be concentrating on returning to my family and re-establishing my career but leaving Frat Gang in good hands weighed heavy on my conscience. Of course, Stanley had no interest. "Man, hell no, I'll pass." I decided on Gilligan and Irish, they both had several more years to serve and did an amazing job working on Willie's case, so I know that they cared about people. They thanked me. "Sure, thanks mate." "It'll be a real honor, Cornell." Over the next few weeks, it felt like I was a retired old man with nothing to do. Staying busy was how I was able to make the past few years fly. I became so bored that I read the magazine articles over and over again because each time they seemed to have gotten more entertaining.

But some unexpected excitement came my way as I sat in my cell one afternoon meditating. Dexter entered, then barked, "Hey man do you have some sort of problem with me?" Stunned, I paused, then politely asked, "Huh, no but what made you ask that?" "Well, I think clearly you do." "Dex, I'm really confused right now, what are you talking about?" "Ok, why wouldn't you choose me to take over the fraternity and I'm your cellmate?" I honestly was lost for words because I truly just didn't like Dexter, I tolerated him. He continued, "I just heard that you chose those two white boys. Do you know how bad that makes me look?"

I then got upset and replied, "No, I don't know how bad that's going to make you look because I wasn't thinking about you at all. I made my choice, just like I made a choice to have you as my cellmate." He just stood and looked at me then got defensive. "You have a real smart-ass mouth, keep it up and we're going to fight, so the parole board can give you six more months to figure it out because I don't think you're ready to go home yet." Glad I paid attention in my psychology course. Dexter was clearly having separation anxiety and trying to intentionally get me into a fight with him so I couldn't leave. I gave no reply and immediately jumped off the bed and hit the emergency buzzer. When the door opened, I ran downstairs and saw the unit counselor Mr. Smith. "Smith, you need to get this guy out of my cell, right now." "Cornell calm down, what happened?" "He knows that I'm about to see the parole board and he's trying to intentionally get me into a fight with him." "Oh my gosh, are you kidding me?" "Look if they're no more cells available, you can put me in solitary confinement until it's time for me to leave. Just please, get me away from this idiot." "I can't put you there because that's almost a guarantee that you won't be granted parole but sit in my office, I'll check something." "Ok." I sat patiently, gazing at Smith as he checked his computer. "You're in luck, there's actually a bed that's open, you can move in right now." I quickly gathered all of my belongings and did just that, leaving that wacko by himself. Feeling defensive, more so juvenile, Dexter then felt the need to spread a rumor that he kicked me out of the cell after catching me masturbating. This guy was a certified clown. My new cellmate Freddy, an older black guy, just slept all day, so we got along pretty well. "Hey Cornell, they moved you over here now?" "Yeah, sorry to wake you." "You're ok, well make yourself a home. I'm going back to bed." For the remainder of the time that I was there, I never spoke to Dexter again.

CHAPTER 19

Success Rate

BY THE TIME I graduated college, several years had passed since the economy had recovered from a recession. I was fortunate to have landed a job interview at the criminal justice center, attempting to start my career as a probation officer but other graduates weren't so lucky. According to www.epi.org, "The Class of 2019 still faced real economic challenges, as demonstrated by elevated levels of underemployment as well as worsened wage gaps for women and African American workers. Fewer than one-fifth of adults ages 21-24 are college graduates. Women in this age group are more likely than men to have a degree. Among 22-year-old degree holders who found jobs in the past three years, more than half were in roles not requiring a college diploma." A labor economist for the Center for Economic and Policy Research in Washington said that many graduates have traveled nontraditional pathways to find employment in their desired fields. Some students started doing unpaid internships at local facilities. Right before my arrest, I recall some new grads being in complete disarray but eventually persevered. "After sending out forty job applications this week, I was able to network my way to a paid position at another company that wasn't exactly what I wanted." But some students eventually landed their "dream job" and are extremely fortunate. I recall hearing that one out-of-state student applied to a hundred and twenty jobs and still couldn't find work. The young and educated are settling for jobs they wouldn't have accepted a decade ago.

While graduates today are more likely to get jobs, they're unlikely to get a job that they are qualified for or in their area of expertise because it's such a buyer's market for employers. They get graduates who will work for less money and for more hours. Young people are also getting off to a slower start. They are delaying homeownership and some big-ticket purchases because of student debt and underemployment. Most Economists agree that "It's not a slam dunk that you will come out after college in better shape than before you went in."

In June 2018, Forbes reported that "the total US student debt was $1.52 trillion and 44.2 million people owed debt. The average student debt was $38,390 and 2% of borrowers owe $100,000 or more." There were many students that held several part-time jobs before finding a position with a company. Some students decided to keep the ball moving and complete their master's degree at night. But after graduating, the average debt in 2019 for grad students is around $45,000. According to www.investopedia.com, "The total amount of outstanding student loans reached an all-time high in 2020, at $1.6 trillion, with the average debt being $37,500." So the past few years have been pretty rough for most college students. Some students admitted, "Some of my job choices have been more out of desperation and to pay the bills, finding a job that gets you the income you need and the type of career you want is a fairytale for people fresh out of college." One most important fact is, you must certainly love your job or you're going to hate waking up in the morning and remain living in complete misery. So, I thoroughly advise those who are undecided about their career choice to remain undecided. Simply start off by taking all general courses such as Math, English, and Science because even if you decide to be a clown, you're still going to need those courses, so there's no need to rush in making a decision. You will remain competitive when it's your turn to graduate but choose wisely. Let's be honest, everyone would like a fair opportunity and wants to make money. According to CNN money USA, graduates who majored in agriculture, construction, or nursing are dominating the job market. Their unemployment rates are 2% or lower -- less than half the national average of 4%. Recent grads with nursing degrees make about $76,000 a year. Having a Bachelor of Fine Arts degree will earn you around $54,000 a year. The employment of fine artists is projected to grow 6% from 2018-2026, about as fast as the average for all other occupations. According to PayScale. com, "An annual wage for people with a B.A. in Philosophy range from $37,000-$83,000." For Welders, the site also states their salary range is $23,000-$63,000. Welders were a hot topic during the 2016 Presidential debate when hopeful Florida Senator Marco Rubio said, "Welders usually make more money than philosophers. We need more welders than philosophers." A CNNMoney analysis found that to be untrue. For new Liberal Arts graduates, overall, the median wage is $32,000 a year. Many Americans have feared during and after the recession that college grads were not finding work or were settling for less working jobs that didn't require a college degree, or as economists refer to them: underemployed. About 44.1% of recent college grads are underemployed in their first job. According to the New York Fed. "That may sound high, but it's not unusual. The underemployment rate was slightly higher back in 2004 (44.6%). It's important to note that underemployment doesn't always mean a bad job. About 36% of young college grads are in jobs that don't require a college degree but make over $45,000 a year which is above the average wage for all new grads.

Robert J. LaBombard, the CEO for Grad Staff, Inc., says graduates miss out on opportunities because smaller companies don't have the resources to recruit on campus, and college career counseling hasn't kept up with an evolving job market. His company provides a college recruiting program to help hiring companies fill entry-level positions. He provides a pretty good example of his company's strategy that has been created to aid the success of students.

"Colleges must adapt to the changing Entry-Level Job Market."

Lauren and Matt graduated from college in 2018. Both had marketable degrees – Lauren in marketing and Matt in business management. Lauren started a job right after graduating, but it wasn't the right fit and she was back in the job market after a few months. Matt was active in his job search before and after graduating but struggled to get interviews and find the right fit. By 2019 they were frustrated and discouraged. Ultimately, both sought outside expertise and with the right guidance, landed management trainee positions with a medium-sized firm specializing in technology and healthcare equipment financing. Lauren and Matt love their jobs and readily admit they would never have found this opportunity on their own or through their respective colleges. The experiences of Lauren and Matt are not isolated examples. With more than 4 of 5 new grads leaving college without a job, their experience is the norm for the vast majority of new grads. However, after a decade and a couple of years after the recession, our economy has evolved and companies are hiring. With baby boomers rapidly retiring, demographics in their favor, and companies thirsting for technology skills, the market for new college grads should be booming.

I could only shake my head and take a deep breath after reading this information. I then asked myself, if my fellow graduates were having a rough time, could you imagine the hard time I would now have, being a convicted felon, re-entering the job market, with no work experience? Returning home and having to check yes on the box that asked, "Have you ever been convicted of a felony?" Was still surreal. "We have a problem that is so huge, this is like Hurricane Katrina," said Michael Hannigan, the president, and co-founder of "Give Something Back Office Supplies," A company that hires ex-offenders. "Normal market mechanisms are not going to be enough to help all of these people that are coming out of prison to make the transition." A recent survey by the Ella Baker Center for Human Rights found that 76% of former inmates said finding work after being released was difficult or nearly impossible. Nearly two-thirds of the respondents were unemployed or underemployed five years after being released from prison. An African American mid-age male spent one-third of his life behind bars. His first bid came at the age of 16 when he was sentenced to eight years in prison for young offenders for being in a car during a drive-by murder. He was released in December 2009 and within two weeks he found a job working as a warehouse shipping clerk. A big part of him landing that job was being able to meet the hiring manager in person. "When you have the opportunity to sit down face-to-face for an interview, you have more of an opportunity to get a job," the gentlemen said.

But in 2012, after he served three years in prison on an assault charge, his second stint behind bars-he faced another hurdle: the box on the online job applications that told employers he had a felony conviction in his past. While he had seen the box sporadically on applications in the past, it was now everywhere he applied. He applied for jobs as a shipping clerk, forklift driver, retail associate and even contacted multiple temp agencies desperately looking for "Any type of job." No one called him back. He was unemployed for 18 months doing "Whatever it took," to get by, even occasionally "Going back to hustling," he said. He finally landed two part-time jobs, one working security at a fast-food restaurant and another as a server at an Indonesian restaurant. He had just started working at a non-profit organization with victims of violent crimes but he was arrested again for a parole violation-one that he says he was not aware of. In August 2018, soon after he was released, the guy started working at The Ella Baker Center as a criminal justice advocate. "Many employers have a mental block against hiring people with criminal records," said Philip Genty, the Director of the Prisoners and Families Clinic at Columbia Law School. "You can almost look at incarceration as a contagious disease," Genty said. "Once somebody has that taint, they are just looked at differently. It's not even at the rational level."

Hannigan of "Give Something Back Office Supplies" said, "Many employers assume that everybody that comes out of prison is Charles Manson," when the opposite is often the case. Researchers from the Harvard Kennedy School who followed 122 men and women who had been released from the State Prison in Massachusetts found that six months to a year after their release, just over half of the group had found a job. Data from the New York State Division of Parole showed that only 36% of able-bodied parolees who had been out of prison for 30 days or more were employed in 2018. The issue of finding employment for those with criminal histories is further compounded by race, especially because black and Latino men represent 59% of the 1.6 million men in U.S. prisons.

In addition, research by Devah Pager, the author of *Marked: Race, Crime, and Finding Work in an Era of Mass Incarceration*, showed that white job applicants were more likely than blacks to get a response from an employer, regardless of whether the white applicant had a criminal history. Perhaps most striking was the finding that whites with criminal histories were more likely to be called back by an employer than blacks without a criminal history. Over the past few years, efforts to ban questions that ask about a job applicant's criminal history have gained bipartisan support and steady momentum around the country. So far, 19 states, including New York and California, have implemented policies prohibiting employers from asking about an applicant's criminal record. The efforts are mainly directed at getting people with criminal backgrounds to that critical face-to-face interview before a background check is conducted and weeds them out of the running. Criminal justice advocates say it's an opportunity that many people with criminal records find hard to come by today. Having a criminal history can sometimes make it feel like "Your application goes into a black hole," they said. Which is basically the garbage can. Broadly, employers cannot discriminate against people with criminal backgrounds, said Michelle Natividad Rodriguez, a Senior Staff Attorney at the National Employment Law Project. But if a former inmate feels they have been discriminated against because of their criminal history, they may have a hard time filing a lawsuit against the employer unless they can prove a racial bias," Rodriguez said. I personally think that the "Banned the box Rule" is a spoon-feeding tactic. I understand that it has helped a lot of people but in most cases, especially mine, even if the box is banned the employer will still be able to see the individual's crime after conducting the background check and pass on the prospective candidate.

Back in 2013, the Equal Employment Opportunity Commission filed a lawsuit against BMW alleging that black workers were being disproportionately screened out of jobs at the auto maker's Spartanburg, South Carolina, production facility due to criminal background checks. After hiring a new contractor to take over logistics at the facility, BMW required the contractor to perform criminal background checks on all employees who re-applied for their jobs. The screening excluded from employment anyone who had been convicted of either a misdemeanor or a felony crime, no matter how long ago the conviction took place. Roughly 100 workers failed and nearly 80% of them were black, the EEOC said. The EEOC then announced a 1.6 million-dollar settlement with BMW. The luxury carmaker has since voluntarily changed its criminal background check guidelines. Absolutely disgusting but still relevant today, and the reason for my previous statement that the "Banned the box Rule" is a spoon-feeding tactic because of the continued racist and discrimination that is going on in America. For some former inmates, the answer to getting ahead after prison is to bypass the interview process altogether and start their own business. Defy Ventures, a New York-based organization, offers formerly incarcerated people training on how to become entrepreneurs, including everything from basic etiquette to how to do a cost-benefit analysis, said Catherine Hoke, Defy's Founder and Chief Executive. Participants then compete for funding in a "Shark Tank" style pitch session. Hoke said, "The program aims to help formerly incarcerated people transform their illegal hustling skills into a legal hustle using entrepreneurship as a tool." At a recent Defy pitch session in a New York City loft, a former inmate who served five months in prison, stood in front of a panel of tech executives and entrepreneurs and pitched her business idea: a food truck selling gourmet waffle sandwiches.

Another former inmate, who served two and a half years, wanted to start a hair weave distribution company. Another former inmate, who served six months, had an idea for a shuttle service that would help transport families visiting loved ones in prison. The judges listened intently to nearly two dozen pitches. They offered advice on how to make the pitches stronger and pressed participants with questions like what they expect in revenue and how their business would stand out against competitors. Such no-nonsense training has helped Defy build and get funding for 112 businesses, said Hoke. One of the biggest success stories to come out of the program is ConBody, which offers fitness boot camp classes. ConBody was created by Coss Marte, a former drug dealer and Defy Ventures graduate who modeled his fitness program on the workouts he did while in prison. Like many Defy graduates, Marte employs other ex-offenders as trainers. "That's what gives me the most joy," said Marte, who has been running his business for 20 months. Yet, he admits, running a business can come with its own set of challenges especially for some former inmates who may not have the discipline needed to keep their business going. "It's not for everybody," Marte said. "Some people just need a job." It made more sense to me that some employers may choose the ex-con over the college student and pay the ex-con less and save the additional money then invest it back into the company, or some employers could hire two ex-cons for the price of one college student. There would be a hurdle but I had a degree so I had a fighting chance and was still marketable in other areas of my field. My options were, working in a homeless shelter for adult men, a group home for juvenile boys or adult males, or an in-patient and out-patient drug and alcohol treatment facility. So, I couldn't wait to return home and be highly productive.

Even after serving time for a felony conviction, former inmates can remain legally bound to the judicial system for the rest of their lives due to court-imposed fines and fees related to their crime. Some jurisdictions are even sending people back to jail solely for their indigence, for their inability to make payments on their fines and fees. "I owed an astonishing amount of $70,000 when I left and still owe money," says a former inmate, who was released in 2017 after serving 11 years for racketeering. "If I didn't have a support system, I don't know how I could have dealt with it." A female that was recently released, recalled during sentencing for her first drug felony, the lawyer she refers to as her "public pretender." She was released from prison with approximately $18,000 in debt. It's a third of which was for "meth cleanup fees," though she never cooked the drug herself, she said. Her husband, separately, owes an ungodly amount of $104,500 in fees, interest, and victim restitution for a burglary. That's almost triple the amount of debt a college student owes after graduation. Combined, the new Bonnie and Clyde couple pays at least $240 dollars every month toward their LFOs (Legal Obligation Fees). "I pay that before I eat," the woman said. Another former inmate had a victimless crime, no one was assaulted, no property damaged or stolen, but owes his State of Washington $14,000 in fines and fees. The state's annual interest rate on judgments is a borderline of 12%.

Another former prisoner was at the end of a three-year sentence in a Florida State prison when he was caught stealing potatoes from the prison kitchen. As punishment, he was sent to solitary confinement with a cellmate who, according to court filings, was "severely mentally ill." The mentally ill man attacked the potato stealing inmate in a violent rage, ultimately gouging out one of his eyes. When he got out of prison one month later, he sued the Florida Department of Corrections for negligence. Instead of compensating the man, the department responded with a counterclaim or a "Cost of Incarceration Lien" of $54,750 dollars which is the total cost of his 1,095 days, stay in the prison at $50 dollars a day. Such cases stem from a Florida law that allows the state to charge inmates $50 dollars a day to cover the costs of their incarceration. According to a spokesman at the Florida Department of Corrections, "Every person who is convicted in the state immediately begins accruing the $50 dollar a day, cost of incarceration. If an inmate sues the department, as this guy did, the department can decide to charge them for the cost of their stay." Wow, unbelievable.

"We're seeing it all over, medical co-pays, cost of insane incarceration claims, you name it," said Randall Berg Jr., the Executive Director of the Florida Justice Institution. Mr. Berg served 40 years as the founding Executive Director and retired in 2018. Unfortunately, Mr. Berg passed away in 2019 after a long battle with ALS (Amyotrophic Lateral Sclerosis) also known as Lou Gehrig's disease. A recent report from the Brennan Center for Justice at the New York University School of Law found that these types of fees, where inmates can be charged for room and board, JUST LIKE IN COLLEGE, have been authorized in at least 43 states. In 2018, for example, an appellate court in Illinois ruled that a Chicago inmate would have to pay nearly 20,000 dollars to the Illinois Department of Corrections for the cost of his incarceration. According to Alexes Harris, the author of "A Pound of Flesh: Monetary Sanctions for the Poor." Ms. Harris spoke with one woman who was a victim of domestic violence and spent eight years in the prison system for shooting the father of her son. She'd been assessed $33,000 dollars in fines but despite the minimum monthly payments she made, the interest rate had brought her debt to $72,000 dollars. That's just crazy. Ms. Alexes stated, "The fines from this criminal justice system, reinforce poverty, destabilizes community reentry, and relegates impoverished debtors to a lifetime of punishment because their poverty leaves them unable to fulfill expectations of accountability." When I was released from prison my cost and fines totaled $4,000 and I had no plans on giving them a penny. However, I have made several payments just to keep my probation officer off my tail. I finally hired an attorney and had all fines and fees waived by the courts. I just find it incredibly amazing how the courts continue to rip people off, when in all actuality the legislators and judges, who uphold these suppression laws are the real crooks and should be thrown in jail with costs and fines that equal their take-home salary. How do you expect someone to pay a fine when you've tarnished their record with a felony then have them thrown back in jail because they can't pay? If the lawmakers were intelligent, they would simply double or triple the jail time for heinous crimes but wipe the slate clean for lesser felony offenses, so folks can find respectable employment after their prison sentence is complete. According to the latest estimations, ten million Americans collectively owe more than 50 billion dollars in costs and fees that were accumulated through the criminal justice system. But some people on social media expressed no sympathy, "They chose a life of crime, so how are their debts and problems our problem?" "They didn't go to school, learn a trade, or get a proper job. They chose the easy way. Which turns out to be the difficult and hard way." "Oh well, tough luck." "To hell with them all, they'll repeat again, and we'll have one less loser on the streets." According to LawStreetmedia.com, the average debt for inmates is $14,000-$25,000 dollars for those who were convicted of drug-related charges.

CHAPTER 20

Right to Vote & Revoked

BACK IN 2008, the historic Presidential Election took place on my birthday, November 4th. I had never heard of the young African American, Senator Barack Obama before he pursued the Democratic Nomination against then-Senator and Former First Lady, Hillary Rodham Clinton. I'm from a pretty tough neighborhood of West Philadelphia. It's mostly populated with African Americans. But on that day when Senator Obama made his way to West Philly, I was surprised to see so many white people pack the streets of my neighborhood. Shocked at the predominantly Caucasian turnout, I fought my way through the crowd to get a visible sight of the hopeful president that went on to defeat the highly favorable Former First Lady for the nomination. He provided confirmation during his speech, "We don't ever back down from a tough fight." But he had my city wrapped around his fingers that drenched him with our full support. The young Senator with a funny name was referred to as cool, and provided a fresh concept of "Hope for the new generation." He dominated the young voters with his catchy slogan, "Yes we can," "Yes we can." I remember seeing those college students carrying signs, wearing t-shirts, and handing out flyers, encouraging people to exercise their right to vote. Barack Obama was able to gain the trust of those young college voters, most of whom had never voted in their lives. They turned out in record numbers, volunteered, and put their lives on the line by coming to my neighborhood, late in the evening and knocking on doors attempting to register people to vote. I recall watching an interview when Obama was asked, "Do you think America is ready for a black President?" I thought to myself, such an indirect racist question. However, Barack's answer won my vote because up until that time, I was on the Hillary bandwagon due to her popularity and work as a Senator in New York.

Barack replied, "If I'm not elected president, it's not because I'm black, it's because I haven't proven myself enough to the American people." Barack was absolutely flawless, and he had to be. His beautiful wife Michelle and their two angel daughters were all perfect. They couldn't find one dirty string of hair in their background. No extramarital affairs, no abortions, no tax evasion, not even an unpaid parking ticket on the young black man. They couldn't even pay anyone to come out and tell a lie on his family. They were absolutely perfect. So, on that chilling autumn evening, Lloyd and I cast our votes on the school's campus. I said, "Since they're both basically proposing the same agenda of lowering the unemployment rate, better health insurance, and safety for the country, the big question in this election is, do you want the first black president or the first female president?" Lloyd replied, "Yeah Nell, he's got me sold. It's actually my first time voting. I never really gave a damn, until I heard Barack speak." I then admitted, "Yeah, it's my first time too." Of course, Vanessa was sprung on Hillary, "Well sorry to disappoint you both, but it's a woman's country and Hillary is going to prove it." Lloyd decided to irritate Vanessa. "The hell with that, I only like a woman in charge and telling me what to do when we're in the bedroom. Hahaha." She harshly replied, "You're such an asshole." Everything was going well in the election until Barack's Grandmother, Madelyn Payne Dunham who was 86-years-old, passed away, peacefully in her sleep after a long-fought battle with cancer. However, she was able to watch down from heaven, while tears ran down her grandson's face as he achieved the historic feat and became the 44th President of the United States.

The 2016 Presidential race for the White House was unbelievable. Millions of people highly anticipated Donald Trump saying something unorthodox and were glued to the television and found amusement every time he did so. As my Pop relaxed on the loveseat, he'd often call out for me to join him. "Hey Cornell, Trump is about to have an interview." "Ok, thanks Pop." It was like a movie, as Pops and I sat in our living room eating popcorn while Trump blasted the media, "Where are you from CNN? You folks are horrible, some of them, not all of them." "And you can tell them, to go #@!? themselves." "If you see someone getting ready to throw a tomato, knock the hell out of them, will ya, I'll take care of the legal fees." Trump was a moving force. He dominated social media and annihilated all opponents along with a few pinching insults. "Low energy, Jeb Bush," referring to the Governor of Florida during debates. "I think Ben Carson, the retired millionaire neurosurgeon, has even more low energy than Jeb." He ultimately destroyed, "Lying Ted," Ted Cruz, the Senator from Texas. "You don't have the endorsement of one Republican senator backing you and you work with these people; you should be ashamed of yourself." "I call him lying Ted, he'll even hold up the Bible and still lie." "Crooked Hillary Clinton and I haven't even started on her yet but she's just as crooked as can be." In an attempt to assassinate his character, Trump's opponents leaked an infamous video where the business mogul was recorded saying, "I'm just automatically attracted to beautiful women. And when you're a star, you can do anything you want, they let you do it, you can grab them by the pussy."

At the beginning of the 2016 race, I was once again on the Hillary Clinton bandwagon due to an impressive resume and adding to her illustrious career by humbly being Barack Obama's Secretary of State. As time went on, I saw how influential the Real Estate business tycoon was becoming. I was astonished. After insulting his opponents on many occasions and numerous fights during his rallies, amazingly his ratings were increasing. Being a fan of politics but certainly not a guru, I had to make sense of this. During this time, America simply did not want to be led by a female President. How does a candidate with 30-years of experience get defeated TWO TIMES by inexperienced hopefuls? One who wasn't even a politician. After her second straight defeat, I then asked some females who were understandably very emotional after the loss, "If Hillary lost to a young black man, who was inexperienced and had to raise money in order to fund his campaign, did you really think that she was going to beat a billionaire white man who basically already ran the country with his massive Real Estate Company? Some women had unfriended me on Facebook which was fine. I took it a step further and posted in another friend's comment box and said, "He might shock everyone AGAIN and do a pretty good job." That statement was well received with several "Likes." I was truly inspired by Barack Obama's 2008 motto of hope. For many, my next statement might be a new level of crazy but is being made because Donald Trump is so influential, whether negative or positive and has proven so many doubters wrong. CNN was wrong, the late-night comics were wrong, all of the best political analysts were all wrong.

I truly believed that after his first four years in office, assuming he did a great job, that Trump would still win the Presidential Election if he decided to switch parties and run as a Democrat. Similar to how some vicious prosecutors often switch parties and become outstanding defense attorneys. Whether you hate him or love him, you have to expect the unexpected and ask yourself, "Well what's next?" If such a drastic decision was ever made, he would instantly be labeled as a "Turn Coat" but what an eccentric and bizarre strategy that would be to unite the Country. Again, this would only make sense, if he did a great job and wanted to achieve another historic milestone that has never been done in American History. Punting an apology to minorities, asking for forgiveness for past offensive language, and discontinuing hurtful policies would be a great start. Similar to the one Governor George Wallace made in 1995, thirty years after he opposed African Americans attending the University of Alabama and setting dogs on black children during the civil rights movement in the 1960s. Trump's actions weren't as severe as Wallace's but separating children from their parents at the Mexican

Border and allegations of Housing Discrimination toward minorities is concerning. During the conclusion that women voters would have their dreams smashed because Hillary Clinton, sadly would not be the 45th President of the United States, more awkwardness arrived that night when the disgruntled Secretary did not immediately come out to offer her conceding speech. She made the speech the following afternoon.

Coincidentally, another Facebook female friend was also too frustrated to continue discussing the shocking election with me which provided grounds of proof to why some say, "Women act on their emotions and that's a huge contribution to why this generation of Americans did not vote to have the first female in the office." A few days later, President-Elect, Donald Trump briefly met current President Barack Obama at the white house to discuss doing what's best for the country, while Secretary Clinton retreated to hiking in the woods. Here is the law in the Commonwealth of Pennsylvania, according to the American Civil Liberties Union: Felons who have been released from prison, or who will be freed by the time of election are eligible to vote. Those on probation or parole also are eligible to vote. But nationally, an estimated 5.85 million Americans are denied the right to vote because of felony convictions, according to The Sentencing Project, a Washington research organization that says one in five African Americans in the state of Virginia cannot vote. "There's no question that we've had a horrible history in voting rights as it relates to African Americans — we should remedy it," Democratic, Former Governor Terry McAuliffe of Virginia stated to the New York Times. Mr. McAuliffe further explained on the steps of Virginia's Capitol, just yards from where President Abraham Lincoln once addressed freeing the slaves. "We should do it as soon as we possibly can." But Republicans in the Virginia Legislature have resisted measures to expand voting rights for convicted felons and provoked an immediate backlash.

Virginia Republicans issued a statement accusing the Former Governor of "political opportunism" and "a transparent effort to win votes." "Those who have paid their debts to society should be allowed full participation in society," said in a statement from the party chairman, John Whitbeck. "But there are limits." He said Former Governor McAuliffe was wrong to issue a blanket restoration of rights, even to those who "committed heinous acts of violence." The order includes those convicted of violent crimes, including murder and rape. There is no way to know how many of the newly eligible voters in Virginia will register. "My message is going to be that I have now done my part," Mr. McAuliffe said down in Maryland, Gov. Larry Hogan, a Republican, vetoed a measure to restore voting rights to convicted felons, but Democrats in the state legislature overrode him and an estimated 44,000 former prisoners who are on probation can now register to vote. Seven other states, Alabama, Arizona, Delaware, Mississippi, Nevada, Tennessee, and Wyoming, allow some with felony convictions to vote after they are released from supervision. In Arizona, for example, one is not permanently disenfranchised until that person has committed two or more felonies, after which voting rights can only be regained through a pardon or restoration by a judge.

The personal and political impact of such disenfranchisement can be enormous, voting rights advocates say, "As whole masses are swept off the voting rolls or prevented from participating in the political process, particularly in battleground states or in states where control of the legislature is tenuous. Many of those disenfranchised because of a felony conviction are once again poor, African American, or Latino. But in other states like Florida, Kentucky, and Iowa, people with felony records cannot vote again unless they successfully petition the governor, a process that can take years and end in a denial. That's terrible. (Maine and Vermont allow felons to vote while still in prison). The voting rights topic continues to be a hot discussion and the issues are being addressed by lawmakers but clearly, there's more that needs to be done. I highly favored one comment on social media that, "Financial warfare and big business and big government drew first blood, freedom is free, it takes a lot of tax dollars to turn citizens into criminals and rob them and steal their right to vote so that they cannot help overturn the corrupt system that they were victimized by." But for those who couldn't utilize the 15th Amendment when Joe Biden won the Presidential Election in 2020, hopefully all voting rights are properly restored, so that people can receive an opportunity to re-elect him, or perhaps vote for the first female Commander and Chief in 2024.

CHAPTER 21

Final Rounds

ON THE NIGHT before my big day to see the parole board, I didn't get much sleep. My new cellmate Freddy asked, "Big day tomorrow, ah young fella?" "Yup." He then assured, "Get some sleep, you'll be alright." "Thanks." Anxiety kept me awake, so to entertain myself, I just went over my future plans of returning back to school and getting a great job. I listened to some music which they played all of my favorite songs until I eventually fell asleep. In the morning, they served my favorite breakfast, which was grits, bacon, and orange juice. It was still early, as I sat in the unit relaxing. I was scheduled to see the parole board at 11:30 am and I received some great last-minute coaching from Stanley. "You'll probably meet with two or three people. They'll ask you some basic questions like what are your goals once you're released? Be sharp, because they'll throw you a curveball and raise their voices and say something just to get you to respond negatively. They'll ask you what you learned in all the group classes you took?" "Ok, thanks Stan, I'll deliver." I was well prepared but still slightly nervous. When I walked into the waiting room, I could see that it was only one mid-age black guy representing the parole board. This made me more comfortable, not because he was black but because Stanley was wrong about me possibly facing a panel of sharks, who would be deciding my fate. Minutes later, the young white guy that was being seen came out and was relieved by exhaling and wiping his forehead. I was then called in by the baritone representative, "Hello Mr. Richards, my name is Mr. White and I'll be conducting your interview for parole today." "Hello, how are you?" "I'm fine but for some reason, I don't even have your file in front of me."

I was surprised and waited for him to irritate me by saying, "Sorry, we will have to reschedule" but I just sat there and watched him as he gathered some scrap paper and began to take notes. Oddly, Officer Roam then walked into the room and stood directly behind me. I guess they had some bad experiences in the past and this was for the interviewer's protection. Mr. White then asked, "So what groups did you take?" I calmly answered, "I took violence prevention and a victim awareness class." Roam then gave him a manila envelope. "Oh, here's your file. I see that you had a write-up for contraband. Care to explain?" "Well, I just simply wanted to cut my hair because I wasn't sure when the barbers were coming." "Understandable. Hmm.. college graduate, first time upstate." He continued to skim through the report, then asked, "And what about your friend that you helped get killed, do you have any remorse?" My heart began to pound and my legs began to twitch. I almost jumped across the desk and snapped his neck. I took a deep breath and replied, "Yes, I truly miss my friend, some poor decisions were made that night on my behalf and now I'll have to live with that for the rest of my life but I just don't want to mess this up." He quickly answered, "Ok young man, you'll have my decision whether or not to grant you parole in 8-10 weeks. Have a great day." "Ok thank you." When leaving, Roam said, "Man that guy's an idiot." I replied, "Yeah, but could you get any closer on my ass. Damn." It was now lunchtime and I went straight to the cafeteria and I saw Stanley. "Hey, so how'd it go?" "Man, I only saw one guy, but everything went smooth." "Ok, now it's just the waiting game. You'll be granted parole because it's your first time upstate." I just nodded and remained optimistic. Now exhausted, I just went back to my cell, read the newspaper then took a nap.

A couple of weeks later while relaxing on the unit, something told me to ask Smith to check his computer to see if he'd been updated about my parole status. I know that Mr. White said it would take 8-10 weeks for a decision, but it surely doesn't take that long to say "NO." Smith was glad to check. "Sure kid, come on in. Ok, let's see what we got here." I stared at him with excitement as he checked his email then replied, "Oh, yes and we do have something, congratulations young man, you've been granted parole." "Sweet, thanks, Smith." When I came out of Smith's office, Gus was there eavesdropping again and bugging me about my TV. "So, Cornell, since you're about to go home now, can I get the TV?" "No Gus, you can't, it's going home with me." "But you can buy a TV when you get home." I was happy to see that Charles Sr. and CJ had finally reconciled their differences and they both wished me "Good luck." Stanley was happy for me but I felt his envious vibe because he had gotten hit with a whopping 18-month extension after seeing the board. It was now a week before the real big day and Smith informed me that there was one more task at hand. "Cornell, you need to go around the prison and get the signatures of all these staff members before you can leave. It's a requirement for your release." I took the paper and got right on the ball while making my rounds. The signatures were from the medical office to assure that I was in good health before I left the facility. I needed the signature from Mr. Phelps to document that each class was taken, to prove that I fulfilled the rehabilitation that was ordered by the judge. That was not a problem as Phelps encouraged me to stick with my plan, once I was released.

Luckily there were no disciplinary actions pending against me, so a signature from the housing coordinator was pivotal. Since I consistently went to church, I received the Pastor's blessings which to me was most important along with a group prayer, when he asked on that final Sunday, "Do we have anyone going home this week." I'd seen how others usually ran up to the podium to receive their farewell blessing but I slowly strolled down the aisle, soaking in the moment. I looked back at my Fraternity, as they circled around me and extended their hands upon my shoulders. The Pastor said, "My son, you have been blessed and have earned the right to return back to society, this young man has conducted himself in a manner that only God has instructed. Earlier, Cornell saw me in the lobby and said Pastor, I'm leaving this week, so I made it my business to pray for him because I actually had other matters to attend to this morning. Cornell, please allow God to bless your life with all that he has in store for you, young brother. Don't you ever return back to these walls again. Farewell, young king." On the final night when the last horn rang and it was time for bed, I said goodbye to Stanley and a few others then humbly walked over to Dexter and said Goodbye to him. We shook hands as he wished me well. I then ran upstairs. The process of going out was certainly not the same as coming in. I woke up around 4:30 am, which I was up the entire night. I, along with two other black inmates who were given a trash bag full of clothes to choose from so we could blend in with society. I chose an all-black Adidas sweatsuit. I poked a little fun at myself by saying, "Damn, I'm starting off wrong already, a young black male wearing all black." The other two guys laughed while getting dressed.

We sat in a much cleaner waiting area, where I expected another medal guarded school bus to appear but a respectable Greyhound bus arrived to take us to our destinations. It wasn't the tour bus that I had future hopes of having but I quickly said, "Good morning" to the driver then boarded. The small, smokey gray town seemed more industrial than residential, more historic than modern. I really did enjoy the tour; it was certainly interesting. The ride home from prison reminded me of my final ride home from college. I saw most of those conservative Republican counties. Some who still donned the Confederate Flag on their lawn or on the back of their pick-up trucks. The real estate was far less expensive but probably a bit uncomfortable to live in due to the racial tension that was easily felt. I couldn't get any good reception on my radio, so it was nap time. I don't even remember stopping but when I woke up the other two guys on the bus were gone and I was on the bus all by myself. We arrived in downtown Philly about an hour later on a grey afternoon. I had a few extra bucks, so I whistled for a cab. The bus driver was nice enough to help unload my TV inside the trunk then took off. I was home minutes later. I surprised my family with the new television and we all shared a group hug with mom wasting no time shoving food down my throat. "My boy is home, come on son, get something to eat." I asked everyone, "So is the feeling of excitement the same as when I finally returned home from college?" Mom yelled, "hell no boy, because you don't have to go back." "That was a pretty good question, are you doing some sort of survey or something?" Pops asked. "Something like that but just curious."

My little sister didn't fail to inform me, "Well, if your room is a little messy, it's because I made use of it while you were gone." "Mom, was she in my room?" "Your room is fine sweetie, just cleaner than when you left it." Surprisingly, we then heard another loud knock at the door which frightened my mother. "Oh, no, not again, who could that be?" When I opened the door, Detective Grant and Detective Simmons were standing on my porch. "Welcome home Mr. Richards, may we come in?" Grant asked. Both Detectives then entered my living room as my parents anxiously watched. "And how can we help you this evening?" Pops asked. Grant answered, "Mr. Richards, Kenny finally was caught by the police after being on the run the entire four years. He finally confessed last week to not telling you that the gun was in the black hoodie. Vanessa had also returned and confirmed your whereabouts." My mother was relieved, "Oh, thank the Lord." Simmons then stated, "Right after your transfer upstate my partner and I were promoted to work with the state and we were assigned to look into your prison issues. We're the ones that granted your appeals to the state." I expressed my gratitude, "Oh wow, thank you." Grant then stated, Wait there's more. Mr. Richards due to your contributions to the facility, the prison would like to offer you the vacant position to become the new warden. Are you interested?" I was thrilled, "Sayyy Whaaat?" The entire room laughed then Grant replied, "Ok, we'll take that as a yes. We'll see you back at the prison first thing, Monday morning." Surprisingly, mother then stated, "Well this certainly calls for an addition to our celebration. Why don't you two join us for dinner? There's plenty enough for everyone." Grant and Simmons looked at each other then Pops grabbed them extra chairs and they happily joined us for dinner. It was indeed a life lesson and I wouldn't change a thing except for my friends being killed. A photo of Lloyd and Nate was placed on the wall next to my 65-inch television, as I now sat in my new office, sporting a dark gray, fitted power suit. When I opened the desk draw, I saw a gorgeous photo of Warden Green. I smiled then threw it in the trash and began my new journey.

THE BEGINNING

Recidivism vs Return Student

ACCORDING TO THE Bureau of Justice Statistics, "The U.S. releases over 7 million people from jail each year. However, recidivism is common.Within 3 years of their release, 2 out of 3 people are rearrested and more than 50% are incarcerated again. Many people face obstacles reintegrating into society following their release, such as problems with family, employment, housing, and health, as well as difficulty adjusting to their new circumstances. Formerly incarcerated individuals often have difficulty securing employment and housing because of their criminal history. Additionally, those with certain convictions may lose state and federal benefits, including access to education assistance, public housing benefits, food stamps, and their driver's license."

According to Admissionsly.com, "In 2020, the United States, overall dropout rate for undergraduate college students was 40%, with approximately 30% of college freshmen dropping out before their sophomore year." According to Worldpopulationreview.com, "The United States is number 6 in the world for the most educated nations." According to EducationData.org, "In 2021, the likelihood of a student re-enrolling in college after they have dropped out is low, with only 30% returning to finish a degree. More than 3 million adults returning to college are considered likely to complete their degrees."

The Loner

In college, you have a number of people that either choose to be solo or have been an outcast because of their image and lack of social skills. We've all heard stories about these individuals, more so in a negative form due to lashing out at their peers for social negligence. For example, the gunman that committed the massacre at Virginia Tech in 2007. He was labeled as a loner with folks knowing little about him because he had no friends. One of the major contributions to college kids being loners, roots from some parents forcing their children to make friends or to join certain activities which are counterproductive. The child should be encouraged not obligated. This leads to the child being unenthusiastic about the activity, which results in name-calling from his or her peers. Regardless of the maturity in early adulthood, the individual eventually would withdraw from the social scene.

Being a loner in prison may not be in a person's best interest because they open doors to be exploited. Subjugation can happen to a person that has tons of friends but being a loner in prison is very rare. Normally, being around other people and socializing is the basic strategy to make the time go much faster. The dynamics in prison are far less, which is in favor of the socially awkward. The pressures of starting a conversation and voicing your opinion to others are not stressed, opposed to being in a college setting because there is simply less to do in jail. It's the same routine every day. There are so many different kinds of weird people in college and prison that it's almost impossible not to make a friend. However, it may either be preferable or due to rejection but oddly some loners still seem to draw a lot of attention to themselves due to curiosity from others who are desperately seeking compatibility.

SPECIAL DEDICATIONS

Eric Beatty 61st
Mikey F R.I.P
Raphel Dunlap 61st
Jamahl Browne R.I.P 61st
William (Wakeem) Custus R.I.P 61st
John (Jizz) Custus R.I.P 61st
Julian Madison R.I.P
Stan Bertrand R.I.P

Made in the USA
Middletown, DE
12 November 2021